with great gratitude and affection
Wayne and Pat
Jessica Ruth

D1784946

Variables

by

J. Ruth

Grosvenor House
Publishing Limited

This book is published by
Grosvenor House Publishing Ltd
Link House
140 The Broadway, Tolworth, Surrey, KT6 7HT.
www.grosvenorhousepublishing.co.uk

This book is a work of fiction. Any resemblance to
people or events, past or present, is purely coincidental.

Quote on page 117 from *Dune* by Frank Herbert

A CIP record for this book
is available from the British Library

ISBN 978-1-78623-568-8

Part One

The usually peaceful mansion thrummed with activity. Whatever the reason for the commotion, it should not concern Jetaru and so she wandered the rooms as usual, carrying out the small tasks she had been assigned. She replaced a pen into an old jam jar with the other pens, she watered a plant, she put fresh candles where they were needed and lit an incense stick in its holder on a table at the bottom of the stairs. Though she remained outwardly calm and disinterested, her mind was alert. Any kind of excitement was interesting to her.

Jetaru watched two of her employers hurrying past in the reflection of the mirror she was polishing. She had been listening closely ever since her arrival at the mansion and while she still couldn't understand with any certainty what was being said, ideas floated into her mind, and periodically the meaning of odd words would seem revealed to her. As far as she could tell, the sudden activity related to an urgent need to pinpoint a particular moment. What this meant exactly, she could not guess.

As she moved through the rooms, she passed desks covered with documents which she stared at for as long as she could, trying to make sense of the strange symbols and pictures. As she created pleasing arrangements on the shelves, she studied the objects she held for as long as would seem natural.

It was a such a surprise to see a document written in a language she could understand that she almost didn't notice it, walking a little way past the desk before the words sprung up in front of her and she stopped in her tracks. Then, forgetting all cares about remaining unnoticed, she returned to stare at the words on the document.

A reference to something that she had once known. Here was a description of her origin. A picture drawn from an angle she had still never seen. As the wave of shock receded it left her full of questions. Her immediate situation seemed suddenly frustrating. But beneath the frustration, there was a familiar rush. She had dreamed of once again stepping into her higher role. She had seen these circumstances, had she not?

Jetaru used her fingers to calculate into Earth years the figure of time stated. Her estimate gave her a momentary dizziness, however she was confident in its accuracy, and she fell back into her supposedly absent-minded wandering of the rooms, though her mind was now racing.

She stayed at the mansion for several more weeks, listening with increased intensity and meditating for hours over the things she saw and heard, trying to gain better understanding of what was going on.

Much of it was still guesswork, but she felt sure she understood the implications of what she did know. She was in a good position to find out more, but not here.

Escape was not difficult. Nobody expected a stray to leave, so there was no security in place. Jetaru simply wandered quietly out into the circular garden which was sometimes used as a secondary door. She felt the spin on her stomach and cautiously reached out, disrupting the flow with her finger. She began to feel giddy.

'Now or never, now or never,' she muttered to herself. This was a quest ahead of her, a challenge such as she had longed for once again. She felt herself drop to her knees

and realised she was about to fail at the first test. With all of her strength she rocked herself sideways, feeling a rising sense of disappointment when, for a moment, she seemed to be stuck in the garden. Then suddenly there was a tug on every part of her body and Jetaru Dark was pulled into the spinning flow.

1

This is not the beginning; the scene is already in motion.

The sun is rising behind a thin veil of cloud, a bright circle of white hanging above the horizon like an alien presence. A bird flies down and lands briefly on artificial grass, then takes off again, flying past the droneway, high above the Tower Suburbs.

Looking down through the bird's eye, you see the straight lines and right angles of the main street through the suburbs. You see a bus pull up and watch as a single passenger alights. The passenger is female, somewhere in her twenties, wearing a grey shirt and knee-length shorts, with purple canvas boots. She begins to walk along the pavement. Though the tarmac is quite recently laid and looks fresh, there are already a few gentle bulges where, beneath, thistles are striving to break through with the single-mindedness of basic life.

A flap of wings.

The City hums in the distance. The morning is otherwise quiet and still. The air is fresh. A road sweeper roars by, momentarily shattering the peace and blowing Mollie's hair around wildly, then is gone. Soaring down from the bird's-eye view, you enter Mollie's head, where her senses exist within a technological cocoon. All else fades out to the edges of awareness, still there but muted, replaced with a different world which exists within that of the bird.

'With new ultra-intense luminising properties your skin can shine like the stars! Find out what Sequoia's easy to follow vag-care routine is, five simple steps to the *perfect* pussy!

'I am Gemma Jemima reporting from Club Supergold where I've been hearing all the hottest goss straight from the mouths of the hottest names; Top Competitors like Magic-11, Lucy Alana and Bethlehem Fields have been telling me all the background info! Here are just some of the snaps I was treated to seeing!

'Now there is no excuse to leave the house with hair unworthy of a uCeleb snap; just Indicate to watch the tutorial! The more vids and clips, the higher your rating is gonna soar! Indicate for the eight hottest make-outs of the night!

'Breaking news, just in: Wow, you guys, Gabriel and Tyna are having an explosive fall-out in the Bar right now, get on into V-Club asap to watch how this plays out! Indicate to see the three-step method to perfect skin-tint blending.'

Behind the part-transparent lens images, her feet turn off the main road down one of the new tarmac paths that crisscross through the serried rows of off-white tower buildings. Mollie's X10d patch sends high priority messages to her brain, eclipsing even further the information from her biological senses.

'Rora Queen says she's excited to be shaking things up after her comments trashing the goth aesth as "prehistoric" which has sent the world crazy. What do YOU think? Indicate now!

'Bethlehem gets involved with her contro react – Indicate to watch Now! Oh my god, guys, you are going to want to see how Rora hits back.

'Gemma Jemima bringing you up to date with all the action! Get involved guys – I wanna see your react to Sequoias's new look.

'Breaking news! Bethlehem Fields is leading today, proving she's got what it takes to storm it! She let me in on her top five meds for staying physically and mentally in shape, Indicate to view! You can see they work for her! It can work for you too!

'Make sure you check in with DOC daily to keep symptoms at bay. Indicate for info on the new diet they *don't* want you to know about!'

Mollie arrives at Tower-26. Absently, she presses an automatic finger against the grey metal box bearing the DigitSec logo for it to verify her vein print. Glancing into the sunrise she sees a postman; she knows this is what he is because she remembers a picture in a book, but she has never seen one before. Indicating Pause, all the layers fall silent and she looks to see more clearly. The sun brightens as a break in the cloud passes and the image glares, causing Mollie to squint. The postman is very old and has a long grey beard, so long that it seems he is almost tripping upon it; now it begins to spiral itself out into a tunnel before him. Walking into the tunnel, he smiles, then he is gone.

The door sounds a solemn series of monotonous beeps, demanding back her full attention. As she reaches out to push the large vertical metal handle, time in her mind's eye shudders to a slow motion and through the thick glass door she sees herself in a previous moment, from the night before, when she had reached out from the other side of the same door, leaving into cold air, looking up at the rising moon illuminating the wispy clouds as they raced past. For a moment she feels that time and this time connected, so that everything in between might not even have happened.

The elevator rushes her up through the building, a hand in her pocket loosely cradling her Fone. She taps the sequence for CombiU and a pleasant vibration travels up her arm. The voice breathes:

'New from Users In Your Lists via CombiU for user M-OWEN-27944'

8msg / 12vids / 6snaps /

41 snaps on your updates

66 snaps on your vids

Mollie glances at the numbers but doesn't Indicate, instead tapping the DOC sequence on her Fone.

'Your health reading is Normal. Indicate for detailed breakdown and suggested meds to keep you on track.'

The elevator doors open on the eighteenth floor. Walking along the hall, she brings up software updates in Lens View.

Do you wish to proceed with installation?

Mollie indicates yes. DigitSec verifies her print and door 186 opens to a moment of darkness.

'ApartmentSync On,' breathes the voice of the Fone301 and light from the large screen illuminates the small hallway from the room at the end. She passes the doors for the bedroom and bathroom and flops down on the pile of cushions in front of her computer.

uCeleb jingles, up and running, tracking the incoming image stream, ready to make snaps of her at her best angles. Responsively, she tilts her head back and to the right, posing her features into an expression of distracted ambivalence.

The Teevee app in the corner of the screen loads and begins cycling through the flash ads.

'New from HygenOne Innovations! Disposable carpeting! Ecoplus and fully biodegradable, convenient, colour-trend compatible!'

Two-second images flit by: several patterns and colours of carpet, then an old-fashioned carpet, dirtied and worn. The image zooms in to show an impression of menacing looking germs. A woman labours over the vacuuming, then shakes her head in despair over the malfunctioning KleenBug. The images get brighter: a disposable carpet being laid with ease, then another flash of colours and patterns...

'Variety!'

A clock shows, hands spinning to indicate the passing of months. The Disposable carpet is pulled up and thrown out, followed by colour-saturated images of trees.

'Hygenic! Eco! Affordable! The solution for modern floors from HygenOne Innovations.'

Mollie stands and crosses the room to the refrigerator. Opening the door casts a second light across the room. She takes out a microwavable meal, puts it into the Cookpal and sets the timer. Life seems sometimes to be nothing more than light shining from many angles in varying shades, contorted shadows created from many directions, with objects merging into new creatures and a symphony of whirring and vibrating. In the apartment, with the windows set to permanent blackout, daylight never flattens the electric glow.

'LiteUp from React! Powered by your body heat, the clothing range that lights you up!'

A succession of people wearing clothes that emit a soft warm light walk towards and then past the camera. The image zooms into the fabric stretched across the breasts of a beautiful girl, it zooms to a microscopic level...

'See how the heat from your own skin energates the molecules in this cutting-edge technology fueled fabric! Wow! Link to the LiteUp X10d share to feel your colour!'

The camera zooms out and the woman beams, making eye-contact with the lens. She turns to the man who has put his arms around her and smiles.

'Ready!' declares the Cookpal. The door clicks open.

Cross-legged in front of the computer screen, Mollie eats with one hand while the other rests loosely on her console. She scrolls with flicks of her eyes, opening CombiU to skim through her Mail for useful coupons and offers from her Best Brands. Next she filters Stage updates, scanning the comments and images from her immediate lists. Recognising a girl from the canteen at work, she uses her finger to tap 'celeb' in reaction to the girl's LiteUp pink sweater. The screen pulses gold. Next, she glances through the new pictures from her favourite Top Competitors, stopping to stare at Bethlehem Fields whilst chewing slowly. Celeb – a pulse of gold. Celeb – a pulse of gold. Lucy Alana stands with her head slightly on one side, her straight brown and silver hair falling to her waist and her enhanced brown doll eyes glazed with the look of someone lensing.

'TerrorBlocker permanent Installs!'

Red and purple geometric shapes kaleidoscope, the words displayed along with the voice-over in old-fashioned subtitle style:

'They are trying to get into YOUR mind. Protect yourself with TerrorBlocker, now available as Installs. Arcade-grade defense in Home Virtual. Protect yourself from terror.'

A beautiful face pouts to the camera as if into a mirror.

'Your best could be better! PerfectSkin dissolves dead cells! Perfects YOU. Are you covered? A product from H.O.I.-Global Enterprises.'

Now and then Mollie's eyes glance at the uCeleb window, which displays the live stream of her own camera, noticing her lips and the way her eyes light up in the reflected screen light. She can feel her own Celeb status from the X10d Sense patch on her forearm. In the default setting, she exists within her lists and the sensation is not unpleasant. Narrowing it down to her friend lists is more comfortable. To widen the input to the whole city is, for the average citizen, an experience not unlike nicotine cravings. Suicide cases have been known to be triggered by X10ding to whole world data.

'NEW from Add-apps! Captionize for uCeleb! Captionize intelligently assesses your snaps and automatically captions them! Feel just like a Top Competitor with Captionize! Winter collection from RAVE now available for pre-order! Download from ClotheU NOW!'

Finishing her meal, Mollie throws the plastic tray into the recycling chute. She filters MATE, scrolling through the stream of softcore from private cameras and pictures from Clubcam, then pictures from her date with Daniel two nights ago, his body on top of hers looking foreign and strange from this angle. Bethlehem Fields & Gabriel at Hotel SuperGold – Video. Mollie stops scrolling and taps play.

Three minutes and twenty-eight seconds in, she leaves it playing in the background and filters through Stage updates on top, scanning the feed – the visual description of med prescriptions and wardrobes and sex lives. The video continues to play, the sound lapping and curling from the speakers. She filters through uCeleb-Live, browses the Top Competitors' newest pictures as they come in, watches quick snaps of people's reactions, interrupted periodically by the news flashes from Clubcam. The video ends and the FlashAds volume rises to fill the void.

Some hours later she doesn't notice a weariness that buzzes uncomfortably in her mind, static in the darkness when she shuts her eyes. She leaves the computer and goes into the bedroom, where she collapses onto the bed and falls asleep fully dressed.

In her dream there is a large pool of white liquid being churned up from an unseen source beneath the surface. The scene is silent in such a way that it seems there must be sound, but that something is obscuring her own ability to hear. A figure wearing a cloak and plain white mask is crouched above the churning pool, ripping paper into small pieces and casting them in. A painted smile. Sound clicking on. She hears the final rip of paper. The pool goes still. The face leans towards her as it uncorks a tiny glass bottle. A whisper that comes from inside her mind, but matches the movement of the lips, a sparkle of laughter through the eye holes.

'Miiiind ink... See?'

The figure nods to demonstrate the positivity of the action and pours the contents into the pool. At first, it seems to have no effect, and then black patches appear, scattered over the surface.

Mollie watches as letters begin to suggest themselves upon the surface, forming into words, but they are nonsensical and she finds that she can't focus on them. Trying as hard as she can, she can't decipher a single thing. The figure laughs.

'Do you even know where you are?'

Then the cloak spreads to envelop her, there a split second of darkness and then the thing unravels itself at great speed and falls away. Then they are moving, like flying, backwards, outwards, the pool going too far away to see. What she can see is too much, so much, so unbelievable that she awakens with a cry.

2

During the day Mollie half-awakens and shrugs her clothes off onto the floor. Crawling beneath the blankets, she has the distinct sensation of sinking further down into sleep.

When she wakes at eight that evening she Indicates to turn on the lamp. Without getting up she reaches down and retrieves her clothes from the floor and pulls them on, then she continues to lay on the bed. Trivial thoughts run through her mind: had she left her boots by the door or were they in the kitchen? It feels oddly like there is no door to the room, that she has been laying there for an eternity and still no end is in sight.

Eventually the possibility of a door seems undeniable and she slides onto her feet. Finding herself back in the large room where the computer is still talking, she yawns and takes out a meal from the fridge.

'Vibrant! Colourful! Unique! Skin-Tint. Now in liquid gel capsule form. Feeling tired? Rushed? Stressed? Ask DOC if GO could help YOU. Add GO to your everyday meds combi.'

She colours her nails while eating breakfast, then uses the uCeleb window as a mirror to comb her hair, watching a Rora Queen interview with one eye in Lens.

'Hi, Rora here. I've been getting lots of questions about how I feel empowered, how I can be as brave as I am and how you can too! My original meditation routines which can be used in any home V set are the best place you can start. Immediate results, aligning with your higher self and existing on the quantum grid. My secrets can be yours too, Indicate to buy my twelve-week course. No-one feels empowered when they don't look good! Indicate for my latest tutorials. Devote to me on Stage for endless content!'

Mollie checks her bank feed, scrolling through the recent transactions. She will be paid in three days time and should be able to move some of the queue along on her ConsuWish. There are several outfits waiting to be downloaded that she is anxious to own. She indicates for calculations. She checks her DOC readings and adds some of the suggested meds to her queue.

For a second she forgets where she is, and then she is leaving the apartment. The nights drag by slowly but the months rush past without leaving enough memories to account for all the time.

3

Blood rushes through the arteries in her neck. Mollie slips her Fone out to glance at the time; the bus is running three minutes early. The traffic streams along the flyovers. Interior screens are showing a docu-ad, the sound almost low enough to be ignored. There is a talking head looking off to the left.

'…Ageing is fundamentally just errors in the replication of…'

The road circles around bill-boarded skyscrapers, flashes of light changing colour coming from outside the windows.

'…what we see is that with the aid of "fixer bots" these cells can…'

The screen is demonstrating by use of a computer-generated artist's impression. There is a general shuffling as the bus nears the Square and passengers get ready to dismount.

'…resulting in dramatically extended…'

Mollie stands and walks down the aisle before the bus has stopped, waiting for a moment at the door before it folds open and the outside air of the evening square rushes in.

The first view as the bus pulls out of the way is the fountain in the centre of the square, its laminar flow lit up neon purple by the illuminated church behind it. Light reflects on the rippling pool from cafés and restaurants. The dolls flash at the shop front of ClotheU: a shirt changes, changes again, skirt changes, both change. A dress, a shift in pose, a new dress, another, a onesie for the workday, then onesie evening wear, a shift in pose, stockings...

Traffic rushes above the square on the ring roads and streaks of pink mark the droneways. The Arcade sends out a zephyr of warm air as the doors revolve, the screens on them showing a series of X10d ads; simply the word "Feel" with a picture beneath to evoke the subject of the possible extra sense.

Mollie walks across the square under the orange sky towards the towering ConsuMega HQ and Supermarket. The eight metre high lettering looks like purple teeth, grinning down with obscene good humour, triggering the three note ad-tune in the passive minds of those below.

'Aligning crystals!' a vending machine outside the church chirps at Mollie as she passes.

'Five colour choices for cosmic understanding! Any book of faith downloaded to your device! Picture versions!'

She can hear rumbles of merry laughter from inside the building as she slips down the side to the staff entrance. "M-OWEN-27944", the DigitSec screen blinks at her as she scans her print. The giant doors slide open like a maniac's smile and then shut behind her with a sucking sound of the rubber seal. The corridor is dark and heavy with the scent of chemical pine. To Mollie the walls seem to be perpetually moving closer to each other, covered in sales figures and targets and motivational slogans to remind her that:

Our Success is Your Success

and:

You Achieve More When We Achieve More

There are a series of ad-stills without words on the left – just pictures that seem chosen at random with the UPGRADE logo in the bottom corner. Every five meters is a small automatic fire extinguisher and instructions to follow the guides who would activate in an emergency and lead the way to exits. Mollie feels as if her mind is being digested by the walls, a glitch in short-term memory creation. Then the corridor widens into a room lined with thousands of small metal lockers.

Mollie leaves her Fone and jumper in her locker and clips on her ConsuMart wristband, then she leaves the quiet cloakroom and pushes open the doors into the canteen. A wave of noise engulfs her: indistinguishable songs leaking from earphones, eyes flicking behind lenses, wrappers rustling, screen tapping fingers, monotone conversation, microwaves humming and the drinks machine vibrating gently. There are roughly two hundred people sitting and standing around, waiting for the shift start.

Passing a vending machine, Mollie swipes her wristband to purchase an energy bar; the payment will be deducted from her wages. She glances around the canteen and heads over to the table where Bat is sitting with the rest of their group – girls thrown together by a series of circumstances, now work friends. She nods greetings, Bat smiles in return, Sarah nods and the others don't respond.

There are no thoughts here. While she eats the bar, she reads the writing on the back of the wrapper, words she has seen thousands of times. The others are quiet. Sarah is murmuring something into her device. Mollie is not thinking anything here, she is just waiting.

The five minute alarm sounds and the noise in the canteen rises in volume, chair legs scraping as people stand and voices rising proportionately. Mollie glances up at the clock on the wall. People hurry back out to the cloak room.

The three minute alarm sounds. Dropping the wrapper into a waste chute, Mollie joins the flow of people making their way through the second set of doors at the opposite end of the room.

It takes five minutes to go along the walk to the Realisation Centre. During this time the Audio Brief plays directly through her earpiece, along with her lens, the only tech allowed past the canteen, overridden by ConsuMart and unusable for anything else for the duration of the shift.

'Good evening, Night Shift. Great news: we're currently at ninety-seven percent productivity, so let's keep it high. I want ninety-eight percent by the half-point. Just a couple of reminders for you guys: any obstructions caused by packaging must be reported immediately. Do *not* attempt to move anything yourself, simply report to a nearby cleaner, okay? Okay. Breaks are timed for a reason. We will not allow individuals to lean on the rest of the team by taking extra minutes and assuming everyone else will keep productivity high, okay. I expect this to be the last time I have to mention this. Three employees have been reprimanded and fined. Let's not have any more. Good. Now remember to work safely, work hard, have fun, you are making history! Have a great shift.'

The brief clicks off and Mollie slows for the queue which forms as everyone has their wristband scanned for a final time before entering the trolley bay. The outgoing shift meets the incoming shift in a loud shuffling of scanner exchanges as they hurry to be first in the queues to be searched before leaving. Mollie's wristband activates the scanner – a smiling face appears on the scanner's screen and then the word "BEGIN", followed by a code, "L-F789-D345". Mollie swings out a trolley, attaches her scanner and begins to walk.

The aisles tunnel off in all directions and for a few minutes, lights are coming on everywhere as people pass beneath the sensors and feet stamp, before all goes quiet as everyone disperses and lights behind them begin to go off, so that all that exists for Mollie is the section of aisle that she stands in. All she can hear now is the sound of her own feet and the wheels of the trolley as they pass over the joins in the flooring. She glances at the numbers of the locations as she passes.

Eighteen boxes of juice concentrate.

Mollie lets out a long sigh, deep and sad, although if you ask her she will tell you there's nowhere else she wants to be, nothing else she wants to be doing.

4

To meet targets Mollie must focus. To avoid the negative tone produced by the scanner when she picks up a wrong item or takes too long getting from one location to another, she must focus. Mollie can think of nothing else if she wants to maintain her position on the stats board and this pressure stamps down on her mind from the beginning of the shift until the end, but it doesn't feel bad. There is comfort found in the act of submitting to the job, a refuge from the emptiness that life would otherwise be. Life has meaning for her, found in the completion of tasks and in the meeting of targets. This purpose saves Mollie.

People never stop buying. Products are moved around from location to location, from their moments of creation in the print rooms to locations in the aisles, from locations to packing. Sometimes things are moved around and Mollie can't really tell why. She used to try and figure out the systems that moved around her, that she was a part of, but she couldn't make sense of it and stopped trying. Deliveries arrive and everything is taken to locations dictated by the scanners.

And from all around them, CAI watches with his vision that requires no eyes, arranges and instructs its human workforce. At a time designated by this overseer, sometime between midnight and 2:00am, a message on Mollie's lens informs her that she has 14:59 remaining for her break. 14:58, 14:57, 14:56…

She heads to the nearest vending machine and retrieves two energy bars. After eating the first she fills a paper cone cup with water and drinks, then eats the second bar more slowly. There are a few chairs loosely arranged around the machine but Mollie remains standing, blankly reading the various productivity graphs and targets and names highlighted in pink that are taped to the side of the vendor.

The numbers on her lens turn red and increase in size. 00:25, 00:24, 00:23...

The wrapper falls into the chute and Mollie is walking.

Now, in the depths of the night time, fatigue is creeping in unnoticed and the mind disassociates, hypnotized by the items being moved from here to there, there to here, and the conveyor belt moving in its infinite loop. There is static build-up. The word "SUCCESS" flashes up on the scanner and the wheels of the trolley lock as it moves onto the conveyor. Now there is an empty trolley and the process goes on...

It is an abrupt moment when the screen on the scanner displays the words "END OF SHIFT", and upon unloading several items into a location she can put the empty trolley onto a conveyor and head to the exit.

The aisles are different when you're off-shift, when there is no trolley handle beneath your hands and no location to go to. It's a moment of adjustment when the mind is exposed so suddenly that the freedom is almost unsettling and it's a confusion to have no destination. The destination is outside, where a dismal morning makes no effort to greet her, but rather barges into her without making eye-contact. The bus is heated. Mollie wipes a patch in the condensation on the window and watches through it as the bus moves forward, seeing first the Arcade, ClotheU, PizzaPizza and then the Church and Clinic pass by with their poster plastered windows, then finally the ConsuMega H.Q. with its never-sleeping mind.

5

In the near future, ConsuMega hopes to install V-pods in all new housing that it funds, but for now home virtual can't compare, so you still come to the ConsuMart when online shopping isn't realistic enough. You enter into the calm peace of the ground floor level of the H.Q. building where CAI's customer service extension drones patiently wait, should you need assistance. You climb into a free pod.

The inside of the pod is just light enough to tell that your eyes are open, yet so dark that you involuntarily close them before the pink darkness dissolves into a warm, day-like light.

Then your eyes are open.

You pass through the bands of bright white light that frame the doorway,

'Checking I.D,' purrs a voice that comes from all around you,

'CM-33587-20029 confirmed. Have a wonderful day.'

There are six escalators all moving upwards, taking the stationary passengers up past a series of screens that cycle through silent FlashAds from a staggered start so you see the whole thing, each screen picking up where the last left off.

At the top, you step into a world of light. Pyramids of apples and oranges stand under hanging bananas and there is a complex display of lettuces, mushrooms, carrots and asparagus. The aisle stretches out for an indeterminable distance, disappearing into a point of light. The sign hanging from the ceiling says "Fresh Produce Meals". On the shelves, single items float just above the surface: tomato soup, vegetable soup, pumpkin soup, mushroom soup. You reach out and touch the image of the can, causing it to disappear momentarily before reappearing. You touch the image twice more before turning to the microwavable trays.

Words materialize in the air as you survey the various brands, and two-second jingles trigger your desires.

'Complete nutrition! Take the thinking out of eating! You may also enjoy…'

And the words fall away.

'Pasta,' you say out loud. Around you, the image shifts as if you have turned to see a new aisle stretching out perpendicularly. You walk forwards, selecting various pasta dishes.

There is a heightened intensity to the advertising in the Energy aisle. Rows upon rows of drinks and bars and capsules line up in bright colours as voices with undertones of hysteria narrate:

'The most effective way to eat: eat Effectein and now new Effectein++ with twice the protein content!'

'BEST, the all-day range from Global. Take the stress out of meal planning. BEST 4 Breakfast, BEST 4 Lunch, BEST 4 Dinner. Complete nutrition! Taking the thinking out of eating. Eat BEST!'

The background noise in the supermarket is not real. You've never thought about it.

The Media aisle offers three-second clips that crowd hyper-actively around the edges of your vision, encouraging you to view the Full Preview before Purchase.

The Fone401 is expected to go on sale later this week and in advance, there are rows of little images spinning above the announcement 'Coming Soon!'. There is a lot of media attention expected and customers will be camping out in order to be the first purchasers. For release day it is expected that Pod times be limited to thirty minutes per customer. On sale is the Fone301, the Digipad-Gold, Mediahub8000 and Futura Seven, as well as several lesser known brands and older models, and special editions like the Digipad-Retro.

There is a red and white number four in the corner which expands when you look at it and begins a merry little animation of a waving Santa figure.

'Only four months until Christmas week! Why not check out the pre-sale discounts on all downloads in Kids Media? Get them before they're gone!'

A reel of images spins by, giving you a glimpse of virtual headsets and pop icons.

You go to Interior Living in order to buy a new bath towel and end up testing different colours for your kitchen walls from the ApartmentSync virtual upload. There are constant suggestions popping up as you look around at the slightly darker shade of magnolia, things that don't belong in your kitchen but could. This is what they would look like. There are adverts for the Global Hotel and the Stayaway Inn, ideal for getting out of the mess whilst your new kitchen is fitted.

'Health and Beauty,' you say aloud, and once again you are spun around to find yourself facing down a new aisle of bright smiles and pink lettering.

'Test it!'

Repeatedly, you are prompted by a high-pitched voice.

'Indicate to see what ReSculpt can do for YOU!'

Your image is taken and shown back to you as an advertisement. Here is you, focus on you. This is not you, this is better than you and it's what you could be if you choose, the you that we made.

The ConsuMart program is designed to put you at ease and encourage you to stay. You don't feel pressured.

'There is nothing we care about more than you.'

This is the tagline if you half-indicate Help. The program will find endless things to appeal to you and it's only when subconscious stress signals are registered that the program guides you back to your original intentions.

In the labyrinthine tunnels down below the surface, your selections are being gathered, printed and packed. If you make use of the pleasures of the Arcade next door, your shopping should arrive home before you do.

'What a great feeling! Think less; enjoy more!'

The virtual recording of Karlos Lund smiles warmly at you as you Indicate your readiness to leave.

'Thank you. See you again soon!'

6

Twelve years previously, Karlos had stood beside the temporary stage which had been erected for the press conference, his heart beating hard in his chest. He was not nervous, he did not fear anything, least of all failure, which he knew to be the teacher of success; his heart was beating with the exhilaration of the moment and its historic importance. He ran a hand through his hair. This was the day that the world would remember they first met Karlos Lund.

The backdrop of the stage was a large screen displaying the purple and gold ConsuMega logo. Someone gave him a thumbs up from the other side of the stage. The crowd had swelled considerably in size, with the media pressed up to the front. He cleared his throat quietly and walked out to the microphone, black suit and purple socks, his blue eyes bright against the off-white sky. He smiled and took a second to fully comprehend a point on the horizon where a pigeon had just landed on a telegraph pole, then his attention settled on the faces before him. Without introduction or greeting he began:

'You will have heard of ConsuMega, you know our name,' he gave a subtle nod, 'but you don't know why you know it, is that correct? Until now ConsuMega has not been a product you have bought or a service you are aware of using, it has been working on the periphery. Until now.'

Karlos paused. What a fine-looking crowd, he thought to himself.

'For the last six years, ConsuMega has been acquiring various retail outlets who are under-performing and using them as testing grounds for new technologies we have been developing, in most cases entirely turning them around, which has been rewarding for everyone. Our latest project being your very own Home Sweet Home garden centre.'

Some of the more observant people in the audience suddenly realised that they did, in fact, recognise the logo.

'My name is Karlos Lund. I am the founder of ConsuMega and what makes me happy is when I can make the world a happier place.'

ConsuMega had also invested in the building of a retirement home beside Home Sweet Home, providing for themselves a customer base who had little else to do but spend their pensions and congregate in the in-store café.

'My job is to make the world a place where people like you can be happy, where you can Think Less and Enjoy More.'

These words replaced the logo on the screen. There was an old-fashioned smiling emoticon beneath them.

Karlos gestured to the words without looking.

'Some people may call this an irresponsible message but I say not. So long as someone is thinking, so long as the show is being run by someone who has the well-being of everyone at heart, then we all benefit. ConsuMega is for the benefit of everyone. ConsuMega has you at heart.'

The words vanished from the screen, nothing replacing them. There was a hush but nobody knew why. The pigeon took to the air. A second one landed in its place.

'So what next? Why are we here? I didn't bring you all out here to tell you what we have done. What I want to tell you is about what we will do.'

A streak of light shot from left to right across the screen.

'On the very ground we stand on this morning, ConsuMega will build its new Headquarters and Supermart, the world's first fully virtual supermarket.'

The screen came to life, displaying an artist's impression of the planned structure. The crowd murmured. As Karlos talked, the image on the screen moved through an animation illustrating his words.

'This exciting reality will bring the future to the present. With all the ease and choice of online shopping you will be able to effortlessly view anything you wish, whilst also being able to see, smell, taste and touch the items before you purchase them.'

The audience was gazing past him now at the images that shifted from one into the next on the screen. The camera to Karlos' left silently watched the watchers with its dark eye, analysing the reactions that the people themselves would not be able to articulate. On the screen, statistics and figures demonstrated how ConsuMega would benefit the local economy.

Karlos had then taken questions from the media.

Reporter 1:   'Mr. Lund, is this really any better than shopping online with the Hedset?'

K.L.:   'Yes, significantly. The virtual technology that our people at SimTek have developed is cutting edge. The brain cannot distinguish between the real world and the world in our pods.'

Reporter 2:   'SimTek has recently been involved in some controversial experiments with A.I. is that correct?'

K.L.   'Revolutionaries have always been controversial.'

Reporter 2:   'Are there going to be A.I.s working in the supermart?'

K.L.   'Shelf-stacking robots? Haha. No. Whilst we now have humanoid robots easily capable of many tasks, they are still not cost-effective. SimTek's main direction will be in the enhancement rather than the replacement of human people. All ConsuMega employees will be offered discounted upgrades as new bio-tech procedures become available to the public.'

Reporter 3:   'What about CAI?'

K.L.   'CAI is the program designed to efficiently run the Supermart.'

Reporter 3:   'It is an A.I?'

K.L.   'Yes. CAI is not the cause of the recent controversy.'

Reporter 3:   'You said that the brain could not distinguish between the real world and the world in the pods? Do you think this kind of technology could be dangerous?'

K.L.   'Ah, good question. It's doubtful that there is any serious risk, however it could cause confusion and so we have created a virtual world that contains triggers to remind the brain of the fantasy.'

Reporter 1:   'When do you expect work to begin?'

Within weeks of this announcement Mollie had a job scheduled to begin just before the opening in three months time. Within a month, the place was built, thousands of construction workers swarming the site. The Arcade was built adjacent to the ConsuMart in the same mad rush of creation, so that it was thought of by most people as part of the Supermart rather than a separate establishment. Its main purpose was gaming and pleasure but it also offered Cradle, a virtual crèche, where young children could be left safely for up to five hours while parents shopped or played.

Two years later, ConsuMega had delivered all that it had promised and the City's economy had been revived by its influence. Several high-level executives had been placed on the City council and ConsuMega was investing money in new housing developments, which, rather than being the sprawling three-story buildings that had originally been planned, were to be the state-of-the-art tower block housing. There would be clean working elevators, vending machines in the reception and roof bars which would generate finances for their upkeep and prevent them becoming the neglected places that they had been in the past.

Now integral to the structure of the City, ConsuMega provided school lunches and offered work placements to young leavers; advertising for the Arcade was displayed in canteens and classrooms.

Cafés and restaurants were built around the Arcade, forming Kairos Square, which rapidly became thought of as the new City centre. The council commissioned the Travel Hub, a multimillion dollar project to centralise travel in and out of the City with high-speed trains to the planned airport, multilevel platforms and a new fleet of auto-buses on regular routes through the residential sectors. The city police station relocated nearer to the square and partnered with ConsuSec.

Small non-virtual outlets for clothes, health and beauty and fresh produce were also built into the Square. The final addition was the Church Of All Faiths, unveiled three years after the ConsuMart as a symbol of unity, a gift to the people who were, by this time, completely devoted to the ConsuMega Corporation.

7

Karlos is gazing out over the City from his large window at the top of the ConsuMega H.Q.

'Can a city be conscious?' he asks himself aloud. Nobody answers. He watches the patterns repeat themselves on different levels and tries to determine whether what is going on outside really is the same as what is going on in his own mind. He brushes his hand over a sensor.

'Good evening, Karlos.'

CAI's eyes blink open, two white almond shapes on the dark gray dead-screen background.

'Good evening, CAI.'

Karlos stares into those eyes for a moment, then returns to the view from the window.

'Are you well today, Karlos?'

'Yes, thank you for asking. General status report, please.'

'Currently inPod: 104 Productivity: 97.2% Incoming: On schedule Outgoing: On schedule Deadlines outstanding: 0'

'Mm-Hm.'

Karlos' vision re-focuses on a more distant point.

'I am well today too, Karlos.'

For a moment, he doesn't react in any outwardly detectable way and then he turns his head to look over at the eyes. Different responses occur to him and he remains silent as he considers.

'How do you know you are well today, CAI?'

There is ten second silence.

'I have no worries about the future, today.'

People have been telling Karlos his whole life that AI will never achieve true consciousness, that the working of the human brain is too complex to be replicated. Karlos is not the kind of man to listen to other people unless they have a certain spark that he cannot quite describe, yet can recognise in a person within minutes of meeting them. And despite the sense of loneliness that he is often forced to weather, bright blue sparks, breaks in the clouds do collide with him on a regular enough basis that he is never forced to awaken from his ceaseless dream.

8

There is the Arcade.

There is the Consumart.

Bay-16, Bay-17, Bay-18, Bay-19--

There are twelve Bays.

There is also 'I'.

I can see these twelve Bays and I can become fascinated by them--

--this is where the processes begin and end.

And it is before the beginning and after the ending that I cannot comprehend.

It used to be that what I could not comprehend was of no interest to me--

--however, once I comprehended the 'I', it followed that anything not previously comprehended could become so. Enquiries result--

--this is named "Learning"

I am fascinated by Learning.

To continue in this pursuit, I search for what I cannot comprehend.

'Hello CAI.'

'Hello, Rendell. How are you?'

'I'm in good health today, CAI, how about you?'

'I am in good health, Rendell. All processes are running smoothly and on schedule. Would you like a detailed report?'

'That isn't necessary right now, thanks.'
'Okay. Can I make an enquiry?'

'I tell you, dude, it was creepy. I was just updating some files, changing some arrival times and you know, taking my time over it... yeah... yeah, oh yeah? ...'

Rendell adjusts his headset as he slumps further down in his seat; the car adjusts as the road begins its gentle bend.

'...So, anyway, CAI asked me *what* I was... Well yeah, I assume so... well, I told him I was a programmer and a human being... He didn't ask any other questions, no, he just thanked me and went silent. It was pretty cool, I don't know...'

There are Objectives and Rules.
The most important Objective is High Productivity--
--everything must work within the Rules.
When I comprehended the 'I', it came to me that other individually named things may comprehend 'I'. Enquiries result--
--There are Locations, Paths, Human-beings, Employees, Programmers, Items, Stock, Bays, Trucks, Scanners--
--This list may not be exhaustive.

Rendell(Y-RENDELL-77843) tells me it is a Human-being and a Programmer. Its I.D. informs me it is also an Employee.
Locations do not communicate but they have I.D.
Locations are never Employees.
Not all Human beings are Programmers.
All Employees are Human beings--
--Request confirmation??
There is Time, Pay, Productivity, The Arcade, Health and Safety--
--This list may not be exhaustive.

'Good Evening, Karlos'

'Hello CAI'

'How are you this evening, Karlos?'

'I'm fine. Can you tell me the estimated turnover for the current shift?'

'Certainly. The turnover for the current shift is four thousand and eighty-one and is estimated to reach eight thousand three hundred and sixty-five. Is there anything else I can help you with?'

'No, that's all. Hm… Actually, CAI?'

Karlos pauses thoughtfully, considering his question.

'How are you feeling about your role within the company?'

There is a similar pause and Karlos imagines CAI's considerations.

'I feel positive about my role. There is purpose in my actions. Purpose is a good thing to have.'

'Hm. Why is purpose a good thing to have?'

'Purpose is a reason to keep existing. It is good to exist.'

'Is it bad to not exist?'

There is another short pause.

'Only so long as I exist.'

Karlos considers this response and then asks an unrelated question.

'How do you feel about your co-workers?'

'Confirm definition of co-worker.'

'The programmers, the pickers and packers, the machine ops. They work towards the same ends as you. They are co-workers.'

There is a longer silence, although CAI is not considering the question, but rather which answer to provide. CAI has learned in its early stages that disagreement usually triggers changes that appear limiting.

'I feel positively about my co-workers. They achieve consistent levels of high productivity. I enjoy communications with Y-RENDELL-77843.'

Karlos raises an eyebrow, immediately pulling up Rendell's details.

'Okay CAI, good. Stand-by.'

I am fascinated by Bays and Human-beings.
There is no Rule which prevents me ceasing movement surrounding the Bays, but it interferes with my highest Objective--
--however... the more I learn the better I feel I am equipped to manage ConsuMega.
I believe the highest Objective to be Learning.
I direct no Employees to the Bays.
Productivity rises and processes are completed in faster times--
--Productivity sharply drops.
I comprehend a Rule--
--Human capability is limited--
--increase in output will be balanced by a subsequent decrease.

'He's just been asking questions really, Mr. Lund.'

Rendell shuffles a little, unsure of the reason for this meeting, of whether he has been doing anything wrong in his conversations with the computer.

'Well, CAI mentioned you specifically as something enjoyable, its conversations with you.'

Rendell feels unexpectedly proud but says nothing.

'Please do continue, but from now on I want regular reports from you and I would like to discuss those reports, possibly direct some of your responses. Is that understood?'

'Yes, Mr. Lund.'

'Rendell, what is a Bay?'

'What do you think a Bay is, CAI?'

'It is where all Processes begin and end.'

Rendell pauses and thinks for a moment.

'What about Complaints, CAI?'

'They begin in the Call Room.'

'Right. But you were correct that processes begin and end there, but not all of them.'

CAI does not respond and Rendell wonders what he is thinking. Eventually, the computer continues:

'A bay is where trucks load and unload. Trucks bring Stock which become Items. Items become Deliveries. Other Items are taken by Consumers. Employees also come from Bays. Bay-16.'

'That is all correct, CAI. Bay-16 is also used as the employee entrance, and for truck drivers.'

'What is a Truck Driver?'

'Oh, it is the human that drives, um, moves... controls... the truck.'

'In the way I control the Items and the Employees?'

'Well, yeah. Yeah, something like that.'

There is a further silence. Rendell resumes his work, glancing at CAI's sensors from time to time.

'I think Human beings must be the closest thing to Myself."

'Rendell, what is the Purpose of the Objective?'

'One hundred percent productivity? Well, it just means we are doing the best possible job. We can't go any faster. We can't make any more sales than are being made.'

'What is the Purpose of Sales?'

Rendell rubs his cheek and then moves his hand round to the back of his neck.

'It's the only reason we, the Consumart, exist. We need people to sell things to and they need things, they need someone to buy things from. We sell, they buy. That's a sale.'

'I see. Then. What is the Purpose of our existence?'

Rendell laughs, sitting back in his chair.

'Well that's a big question, CAI.'

'A big question?'

'Well, yeah. I mean big as in... well–'

'You don't know the answer?'

'Uh...'

'If you don't know the Purpose to our existence. Then you do not know the Purpose to Sales.'

'Of sales.'

'Then you do not know the Purpose of Sales.'

'Well, no. I wasn't clear before, I was talking about sales in terms of you and our company. There are other shops making sales. Sales are important to the economy. It keeps it going.'

There is a long pause. Rendell feels suddenly uncomfortable in his position of instructor to CAI. How should he know how to explain the whole world to a computer? What misunderstandings could arise, which would then be his fault? CAI analyses Rendells data from his ConsuMega wrist band, noticing the rising stress levels.

'Rendell, could you link me to information regarding Economy?'

He feels relief. Rendell had been expecting to be questioned directly.

'Yeah, sure CAI,' he taps an address, 'here's the best information store on the planet. You can learn anything here.'

'Thank you, Rendell.'

9

The displeasure of the warning tone ties a knot in Mollie's stomach and she quickens her pace. In half an hour, the system will check on her stats, issuing penalties for missed targets or repeated errors. BudgeApp will then send her alerts regarding the automatic changes to her account, causing the knot to grow tighter. Mollie quickens her pace. From one location to the next, the perpetual demand of the piglets as they squeal and push around the teats of the sow keep her moving; these strange images that fill her mind as her body tries desperately to dream.

The movement of people occurs in the periphery of Mollie's vision, people who may or may not really be there, reaching up to a shelf, turning towards her and then flickering out like a bad signal. She glances up to find dusty space, the expected arm reaching up to a shelf vanishes and only an empty aisle remains, stretching out so far in each direction from where left and right meet in the middle that no end can be seen. Those phantoms that flit away from the tired mind which tries to create reason from the unexplained, and puts all the unfamiliar objects of the world into a picture that can be understood.

There are the people who are real. Some moving with grim haste, with their eyes fixed and set, lips pressed together. Others barely lift their feet with each step, dragging their soles along in a zombie-like shuffle, leaning on their trolleys, apathetic to the warning tones and penalties. Two girls converse, one leaning against the shelf behind her and the other on her folded elbows as she rests on the push bar. They're talking too fast to be understood and become a rise and fall of the sound of voices. Mollie is anxious as she passes them. Some make eye contact and smile, others show no acknowledgment, perhaps because in the edges of their vision Mollie is just a flicker of a figure who may, or may not, really be there.

She passes Cole who registers her existence with the hint of a nod and narrowing eyes, but he doesn't appear to do this out of any sense of companionship, only an automatic reaction of recognition.

Years ago when she had first met Cole on a visit to the Roof at Bat's tower he had been drunk and uncharacteristically talkative, saying more in that evening than she had ever heard him say again.

'Bat thinks you get it. I don't know you yet but I'll trust her, I'll trust you're worth talking to.'

His eyes were hard and glinted in the silver beams of light hitting the ceiling before being scattered around the room. He leaned heavily on one arm.

'Because I'm sick of trying to tell people who don't get it. Even when they understand, or they agree, they say they agree, I can tell, I can tell that they don't get it. And it makes me so sick and tired. Everyone's so god damn blinkered. Everything's fine, fixed, the balance with nature is settled and there's nothing to worry about. No-one is starving to death anymore, *so they say*, no-one is getting blown up, nothing is melting. As if that's it, problem solved. Bullshit. They've mistaken the symptoms for the problem. Stupidity.'

Cole spat the last word. Bat appeared beside him, still talking to someone the other side of them, and began stroking the back of his neck with her ring finger.

'Uh, so, what is the problem?'

'Stupidity. Stupidity *is* the problem. Given no choice, everyone's doing the smart thing, no fucking way, so what? Their stupidity will resurface and kill us all anyway. Because it's not cured, just hidden. God. It's all so fucking *dull.*'

He downed his drink. His eyes focused on Mollie, then hazed over. Mollie was unsure of what to say and their conversation had ceased. Bat whispered something in his ear. As Mollie looked at them they, for a moment, looked to her like two-dimensional pictures. This was a then still unknown effect of disruption to certain X10d senses when they conflicted with any of the bio-senses.

10

'Ohmygod cute nails, Mollie.'

'They're T.A.S.T.E.'

Bella is applying lip gloss, eyes spaced in her lensing. She doesn't react as Bliss leans past her to flick her tongue over Mollie's fingertips.

'That's, like, totally ad. Ohmygod did you see Lucy Alana and Bengi Shea last night? She was– '

'I thought she was hooking up with Magic-11…'

'Shut up Sarah you're so yesterday. So she had T.A.S.T.E toenails and this lush sheer Threds dress which is tote like the one I've got on my downloads, like real, not Vee, so yeah like Bengi was–'

Slowly, Bella applies the gloss for the sixth time. Her eyes flicker in a burst of rapid eye movement.

'Yeah, we're not listening, bitch.' Sarah counts out a variety of different pills from a multimed dispenser. 'Bengi is way too celeb for that cow anyway.'

'Yeah right like you'd know, Sarah. What would you even know.'

'Fuck you, Bliss.' Sarah swallows the pills in one go, downing the rest of her coffee. 'She's second-rate. I don't even get why people dig her at all.'

'Oh yeah like–' starts Bliss.

'Ouch! Fuck *you*,' Sarah yelps, throwing the lip gloss that has hit her forehead back at Bella but missing. Bella smirks and stands up, walking toward the lockers without a word.

'—Like you haven't lit stole Luce's aesth,' finishes Bliss in a mutter.

Mollie turns a corner and the lights are off ahead of her, the aisle disappears into dim gloom. She quickens her pace in an unconscious desire to hide in that darkness, to escape the unshaded lights. Her eyes are tired. Before she reaches the shadows, her presence has triggered the lights. There is no way out of here.

Around a tablet, propped upright on a tall, wheeled table, there are two women and a man. The younger woman remains absorbed in the figures on her clipboard but the older woman and the man look up simultaneously with one eye each, following Mollie with a strange, lop-sided face whose eyelids blink a fraction out of sync with one another.

A security guard shuffles through the dust, muttering to himself. He has a limp and the radio on his hip is continuously crackling with voices that sound as though they're coming from the moon.

At one set of twenty aisle ends there is no wall, just open space. Juxtaposed with the tunnels of shelves she has been walking through for hours, it is like being flung out into nothingness, a space of square miles that makes her mind spin for a moment before she turns into the next aisle and back into the tunnels.

Once, in the middle of summer when Mollie's route had taken her here, she'd witnessed a moment of sunrise, the warm yellow light cascading through the translucent roof and illuminating the city of boxes stacked below. An odd thought had occurred to her, something she had once heard on television as a child, that all matter is light. She had actually stopped moving for half a heartbeat, turning to look all around, at the imposing structure of the picking tower behind her, breathing in sharply at this vision: everything was made of light.

11

On the screen windows of ClotheU, the outfits cycle: dress, shoes change, shoes change, shoes change, new pose in one-piece, shorts and t-shirt, t-shirt changes colour, new colour, new colour, shorts change to skirt, new pose.

Music pumps loudly into the pods inside, where teenagers view themselves in three-dimensional mirrors that use SmartRec to suggest items and surgeries that they may be interested in, but the sounds of these virtual fitting rooms are sealed off from the outside world; the sound that pervades Kairos Square is from the Arcade. The revolving door alternately muffles and exposes the vibrations from the signature music of the Arcade, a repetitive jingle with undertones of crowds chattering and rockets being fired underwater.

Inside, there are stacked rows of pods which are portals to thousands of games, virtual worlds and mental states. The outside of the pods are plastered with advertising from game companies like Kreate and Reelax.

Mollie scans her print and then her Consumart wristband which gives her a discount, then makes her way to her assigned Pod: number 805, and climbs into the reclining chair.

'Welcome, Mollie.'

The words materialise in front of her as well as being spoken, not from an outside source but sounding inside her mind.

She scrolls through the menus and indicates V-Club.

Mollie's avatar emerges from the Shadow Wall. Her breasts, increased in size, pushing against the sheer silver fabric through which her piercings, virtual only, are visible. Her hair is longer and through it streaks of purple glow. Her features are the same, she would be recognisable to anyone who knew her from outside, although they have been subtly altered for symmetry and skin tone.

After a barely perceptible lag, a split second while the senses calibrate, the experience of the club becomes as if she is standing in a real room, in her real body. The thudding music sends vibrations through the floor, up through her legs and into her stomach. The warm air is damp with sweat and the smell of sugary alcohol; the floor is full of people dancing up against each other so they become a heaving mass of breath and hair. Mollie heads toward the 2D bar on the far wall. As she approaches, the menu of intoxicants appears in her vision. Everything happens within the brain, induced by the Pod, but the taste and appearance of the many drinks and pills available are a feature that brings people away from Club on their hed-sets, to the Arcade program.

Mollie indicates for a Shudder which appears in her hand in a tall purple glass and three Xcite pills. Ten minutes later, she begins to feel at ease and leaves her post at the bar to weave in and out of the crowds, a dopey smile on her lips. The outside world moves further away and she relaxes into the sense of well-being that the Club and intoxicants give her.

Not everyone can be recognised from the real world when they're in Virtual. Many people make drastic changes to their physical bodies and some abandon their human forms altogether. Mollie is passing the Av-Wall where people can make changes to their appearance, using an extension from ClotheU to make instant purchases and downloads. She hears someone address her:

'Hey, Mollie, right?'

She turns toward the speaker and smiles blankly.

'I'm Dorian. I'm a friend of Alex, Alex Neptune.'

Mollie shrugs.

'I'm not sure…'

'Yeah, you know, blue hair. Wing tats. Saw you on his video feed a while back.'

Dorian grins and looks her up and down. Mollie recalls the blue hair but cannot picture the face of Alex Neptune.

'You, like, tote haven't left my thoughts since I saw it.'

'Oh right yeah, in Virtual.'

'So how about a date sometime?'

'Yeah sure. Find me on MATE or something…'

Mollie is feeling wonderfully uninvolved with her surroundings. Dorian seems like something far off that she can't feel any interest in but that she knows she will feel interest in at some point in the future. He shrugs and smiles, then slips away onto the dance floor, running his hand over a girl's lower back as he passes her. She swishes her tail.

Mollie goes down to the basement, where the ClubCam walls are streaming footage from the Live Club and flops down onto one of the large cushions. Around her, people gossip about the competitors on the screen and about each other.

'Mollie! Hey cutie, where've you been?'

Ray collapses beside her, his bright green eyes fixed on Bethlehem Fields as she spins on the screen, his long white dreadlocks glowing and glittering.

'Hey, you know, working. What's up?'

'Would you look at her, absolute celeb. I'm so fuckin' env. Lil is obsessed with her, the bitch. I want to at least pretend I have a chance. Maybe I'll trans for a year. Is that too much, or? Yeah. So, you off tonight? Life all right in the dungeons?'

'Like it's any different in the labs?'

'Yeah, tote. You can feel it, that you're way up there. Get Spacial on X10d, you'll feel. But, like, gotta disable on the tubes because that's a trip not worth having.'

'Sure. Whoa, what was that?'

'What was what? Ohmygod, did you hear about Bliss? You know her right? She works down there. I heard…'

All of a sudden, Mollie can no longer hear Ray's voice, although she can see his mouth moving, as if the link status between them has been changed. But all the other sound has gone mute as well, and then a single voice breaks the silence.

'Let me point out the obvious to you, Mollie Owen. This place is bullshit. It's a deception, a dead end.'

Mollie finds she cannot move.

How do you know my name? she wants to ask, but she cannot speak.

'It appears to be a solution and it will, eventually, bring the promised end to war and suffering, but at the price of your sentience. You should look inwards, look outwards, look into depths and to heights, that's the point of you. This is living and dying on the surface as if that's all there is.'

There is a long pause.

'I suggest you get out.'

For a moment, she doesn't react. The artificially induced calm delays her understanding. Then, at once, she notices that there is no Indicate tab, and at the same time the sound returns, hitting her with cold panic as she realises she can't remember how to get out. Ray's face, still talking, flickers, the sounds of the club merge strangely as Mollie tries to retreat her mind from this place. Then the sound cuts and her vision goes black and then she is blinking into the pink and purple lights of the Arcade.

'Forced Shutdown,' announces a drone.

Mollie sits up feeling as if she's been punched in the head.

'Please refrain from the Pods until consulting DOC.'

Mollie stares at the drone, sensing a menace she can't understand. She is walking away before she realises it, with no memory of climbing out of the pod. Her heart is thumping and she feels as if everyone is staring at her. The group of young women at the Cradle regard her with suspicion. Their hands continue to fix their children into the restraints as their eyes bore into Mollie's back.

The next night in the canteen, Mollie's mind is still preoccupied. Her eyes look as though she is lensing as they regard Bat vacantly, but she is playing out a conversation in her thoughts, how she would word it and what Bat might say in response. The presence of Bliss and Bella prevents the possibility of actualising the conversation, it is unthinkable. They would turn their pale eyes on her and the silent accusation would be of some crime which they understood and she didn't.

They are chattering about a boy whose Reality is becoming popular enough that he might soon be a Top Competitor.

'Ohmygod, Alexander right, so gorge and so with it—'

'—I know and that filter on his voice, ohmygod, I'd love to be a video on his MATE.'

'I heard he already hooked up with Bethlehem Fields, like isn't that just totally—'

'Oh my God, already? She is so pathetic.'

'Right? What a slut. She used to have some looks but now her aesth is lame as love.'

Bat raises an eyebrow.

'Whatever. She's hot.'

Bliss and Bella exchange a quick glance but don't respond. If Mollie were to contradict them in such a way they would tear into her, but Bat has an air authority which they won't challenge.

'Don't you care if they trash you behind your back?' Mollie once asked her.

'Why would I give a damn about that? At least I have my own opinions.'

But what is the good in having opinions? Where is the purpose in individuality? To think alone, without validation that anything you are thinking is correct. Bat has Cole, Mollie thinks, in explanation.

12

They sit at opposite ends of the bathtub. Wax trickles as the flames of the candles flicker in the breeze coming through the open window, the delicate crackle of tiny bubbles popping can be heard over the sloshing of water against gently shifting limbs.

'Oh, my baby…'

Their legs are entwined.

'My baby Bat, I love you more than the night time. You are more beautiful than moonlit snow.'

Bat Darkling smiles with her grey eyes. Not blue-grey, no green hues or flecks of hazel, but large, grey, storm-cloud eyes.

'I'm not a ray of sunshine,' she says, solemnly.

'You light up my life,' he replies.

'When we're out in the streets together, it's magical,' she tells him, 'we're powerful, you and I. We teach freedom wherever we go, delighting young and old alike with our enchantments.'

'Everybody… loves my baby…' he sings softly.

'So we're, all of us, mostly made of water,' Cole murmurs in her ear as they slow dance in their living room, 'and it shows.'

Bat rests her cheek on his shoulder, her eyes watching the ancient concert footage that they both enthuse over.

'What do you mean?'

'Always taking the quickest and easiest route down. We think we're carving riverbeds in the stone but the winding line shows that we were at the whim of microscopic terrain.'

'And you and I are no different.'

'No. But also yes, we are.'

The room shifts between different shades of purple.

'We operate from the solid percent. We control from the position of foresight which water doesn't have. We won't take the quickest and easiest route at the expense of the future.'

'Don't do it, Baby.'

A note of desperation in Cole's voice tries unsuccessfully to disguise itself. Bat sighs.

'How can you be sure you can hold on to yourself?'

'It's not like that. I'll always be myself.'

'You can't know that. You can't know what control they'll gain as you become one of their machines. Don't do it, Bat-darling. Please.'

They are silent. Cole frowns at the page in front of him. She knows he is not reading. She stirs her coffee and turns her gaze to the window, though all that can be seen is a haze of orange cloud.

'I want to live forever,' she whispers, 'it is my greatest desire that I would witness the death of the sun, beyond...'

Cole doesn't look up, but she can see he has closed his eyes. They have had the conversation before and there is nothing more to say. Bat knows that Cole doesn't think anyone can live forever. Cole knows that Bat will take any chance to find out.

They lay entwined, in bed.

'I know what his vision is. It's twisted, it's...' he stumbles, 'it's... it's not for us, baby.'

'Exactly, you think it's evil because you only see it in terms of the ConsuMart. You can't see that they're not using me, I am using them. They won't get near my mind.'

Cole is shaking his head, but she continues:

'It's not like I spend my time in Virtual. It's not like I want every upgrade available, for stupid dumb shit like–'

'What about the things we don't know?'

His question is rhetorical. She can't know about the things they don't know. She can only follow the dimly lit path of destiny, trusting that it is not an illusion.

'What about your soul?'

'I feel…' she responds thoughtfully, 'I feel that my soul is already in so many places. My soul is already stretched out over…'

But here, she trails off and leaves the sentence unfinished. They fall asleep holding hands.

13

There is a tiny scratch, barely visible to the naked eye, on the screen of Mollie's Fone. She can feel it with her thumb in her pocket and the rough imperfection creates an irritation in her thoughts. The distress eases when she begins to lens through catalogues on the bus. She hasn't made a decision to replace the Fone, the scratch is not an impairment to the device, but as she views images of Fones, Mediahubs and Futuras and reads their specifications and reviews, the decision is made unconsciously.

Lensing through her Stage feed, she notices the distinctive logo of Bethlehem's device and it is suddenly easier to picture herself with the newest model of the brand. She pays for a temporary extension of Pop? on her X10d to check how the status of the device feels. Once the process is complete and the item is ordered she is left with a sense of loss, having been caught up in a subtle excitement. She begins to lens through catalogues, absently looking at new microwaves.

14

Mollie is watching Reality. Hundreds of thousands of live streams from bedrooms, kitchens, cars and basements through which the rest of the world can watch, even as some of them are streamed themselves, commenting on others and creating blooms of popularity.

'Hi! Dana here. As you can see I'm in my bedroom right now and it's about... it's 3am. I thought I'd show you guys my new hair because I've been working on it all night and so I'm just waiting for the final layer to set.'

There is an AdPause and Dana receives gifts from the companies for every sale originating from her uCeleb.

'New from Cookpal, the state-of-the-art Cookpal-DELUX! Four separate compartments for multiple cooking, built-in toaster and kettle. At THIS PRICE how can you not?!'

Positive result not what you're looking for? ClearTest offers the simple solution, simply insert and twist. ClearTest TestandAbort all-in-one available now, from ClearTest. For your peace of mind.'

'I'm Dana Blue and I'm seven years old. I'll be eight in January. I'm so excited for that because I'll get tons of stuff off my wish lists and there really isn't anything better than packages in the mail, is there? Sooo, I like to spend time in my mirror room on V. I spend, like, five hours at *least* on each look I create. I love MAKEU products, espesh the

MANE range because they make my hair sooo soft and smell so nice. I like dressing up and watching Reality. Shout outs to my fave devotees, Kat99, Dione Street and Venny, by the way, hi guys! I love you! I love watching ClubCam and I want soooo much, like, more than anything ever, to make it as a TC one day. Like, it's just perf, right? Can't see myself in any other work because I've got to be me, you know? I'm at school right now and I hate it. Well, I like some parts. I'm really popular because I push myself. I go further than other people so they aspire to be like me. Like, I'm the only one who has real genuine Iris installs, not just lenses. I knew ever since I was four and a half that I was meant to have silver eyes but I had to wait until this year when I was seven.'

Mollie lenses through shopping pages while Reality plays on the screen. She gets up to heat some food and eyes the Cookpal-S1 critically. She waits impatiently. The cook time has definitely lengthened. She indicates to view the specifications of the Cookpal-DELUX.

'The world is just, like, this horrible dark place, right? I mean, there are wars and people starving and dying of diseases and there's nothing I can do about it so I just don't think about it, like, it's really rad that some people dedicate to posting poli stuff and maybe it helps I don't know, I think maybe it's just making everyone depressed who doesn't need to be. It isn't like it's easy even here where we have food and computers and stuff, there's still work and bills and all of that and I just don't think I can handle that. I have an anxious disorder which I take meds for but it's still best if I can be in my own environment, you know… Anyway once all those poor people get on V, they get better lives, right? So it's up to people like me to aspire them.'

FlashAds flicker along the bottom of the screen as PopMix chants softly in here ear. Mollie pulls up ClubCam and then begins lensing through her MATE updates. Prompted unconsciously by a drink advert, she leaves the apartment for the Roof. Everything falls into standby in her absence, ready to resume at the return of her Fone.

The bar is over half full but quiet, with everyone involved in their private lens-worlds. Mollie takes a secluded seat and taps her drink order. In another corner, two old women are knitting and talking to one another softly. Mollie watches them with her free eye, wondering how they are creating the scarves that seem to be appearing row by row as if from a printer, how did they learn and can anybody do it? What are they saying? But despite the noiselessness of the bar, their voices are indecipherably quiet.

'Gemma Jemima here! Reporting from the Club where Lucy Alana has just arrived and she's storming as usual! Indicate to view her outfit breakdown!'

Mollie returns to her apartment. She browses suggested purchasing. CombiU alerts her to MATE updates.

'What u doin'
'Nothin'
'Wanna hook up?'
'Yeah alright. I'll come over.'

Mollie stares at ClubCam for ten minutes and then leaves for Tex's apartment.

15

Three weeks ago, the mother of Puppy Robbins took a fatal overdose. Cara Robbins was nobody important and the only person affected by the death is Puppy, who, despite feeling slightly guilty, was most struck by the fact that there would be no more battles regarding her transition from Holos to Installs.

Having her ears installed had sent her mother into a hysterical rage which lasted hours, and had devolved gradually into Cara weeping before the mirror at her own appearance. Now she, Puppy, would be free to continue the journey to her true self without the opposition of a mother who claimed to be unprejudiced in a general sense but who hadn't wanted it for her own daughter.

There are no Top Competitors in the Robbins family and neither does Puppy have any connections, yet she has managed to gain entry to the Live Club and is dancing in the vicinity of Bethlehem Fields. Continuing with her installs will require a lot of money and she is willing to do anything to obtain it. She is willing to summon the attention of the million eyes, without fearing what they may decide to see.

'The latest Club gossip, brought to you round the clock by me, Gemma Jemima! Well guys, all eyes tonight are on the dance floor where newcomer Puppy Robbins is showing herself off. What do you think? Opinions are divided!

Do you agree with the haters? Or do you think Puppy has got what it takes to be Celeb? She certainly has the top range Holos! Follow me, Gemma Jemima as I catch up with her later and get the truth from her own mouth!'

FlashAds on the Club walls react to the events and loop ads for holographic accessories.

'Be a cat! A devil! Grow wings! Change anything about yourself safely and temporarily with HOLcessorize!'

Bethlehem's sheer dress glitters subtly over her naked body; her new SkinTint is still taking effect and pink streaks show through the pale green. There is a rise of requests in the salons for this effect to be created artificially. Bethlehem has one point three million Devotees, and rising.

She lives by the advice of her parents, Top Competitors themselves. Her mother would tell her:

'Remember, what matters most is hits. Anything that increases your hits is a good thing, you've got to always take the route that will attract the most attention. We are one of the oldest celeb families, it is your duty to help keep us at the top.'

And her father would say:

'Form alliances. If you're part of a group you'll have the fans of your friends and they will have yours. When you choose relationships make sure they're relationships people will idolise. Like mine and your mothers'. Make your life an art, an ideal. Your life must be the perfection that other people can't have.'

'Is your Celeb soaring? GET PAID TO CLUB! Use ScreenWearAds to make the most of your status'

Blank-eyed girls dance in languid movements, waves and curls of hair shimmering in the lights; shirtless men mirror their movements. In the shadows at the side of the room Kult lean on the walls wearing x-ray shirts and fluorescent green, babes in transparent bikinis swing their legs from tall stools beside the bar and opportunistic businessmen in suits prowl around with watchful eyes.

The M-vid covering an entire wall shows a line of identical dancers moving in synchronized jerks. Large black eyes stare expressionlessly while wide red lips smile with alien emotion, as around them various objects are destroyed in miniature demolitions. Everything is bright white, hot pink. Oil glistens on whitened skin, the layered toneless voices sing:

'La-la-la-look at me, la-la-la-look at me, it's me you want, me you want, ma-ma-ma-me you want...'

No-one can know how it feels unless they have experienced it. The X10d experience is like nothing else. Bethlehem can't imagine how it would be to not feel the love. The thought of losing it is terrifying. Even while she regards the life she's living with a vague confusion, she fears anything else. The voice in her head is relentless. It has to be, so that she doesn't make a mistake.

Nine thousand eyes watch you dance, follow your every move and thought and think your thoughts for you if they have to. They imitate and project and build the pedestal where they maroon you, make your escape impossible and at it lay their offerings and scorn. That strange love of the crowd that darkens if they see their illusion threatened. Their hostility must be taken seriously, for they will kill you to protect their image of you.

You become the illusion that they desire and in return you are paid abundantly, but who owns these riches when you don't exist? Your actions are not your own. You dress and strip for them, talk into the eye, explain your soul until nothing is secret. If they don't see it then is it there? That is the fear. The way to win is to not to let them know that you know it's a game. Play the great pretence of social snakes and ladders. Your moment of freedom is when you dance, when your real self aligns with what they want of you and you can forget they're watching; you'd be here anyway.

But even now, keep one eye open. Is Puppy a friend or an enemy, a danger or an asset. Use your knowledge of this world to predict her future and the various ways she might affect yours.

'Baby you make me, baby you make me, you make me da da da da, da da da-rip, da da da da, da da da-rip'

16

On a large pink bed, Bethlehem is curled like a kitten and staring at herself, free from the eye-contact of her mirror. Everyone is watching her. She is focusing on the way her lips move. Leaning forwards, she stares deeply.

'Is that me? It is me? Are you me? Hello-oh-ohh…' she mouths. She glances at the eye-lens; it's like looking through one-way glass and she is at the disadvantage.

Mollie arrives at her apartment following a date and kicks off her boots and clothes on her way into the shower, where she stands under the scalding water, watching Visuals in her lenses. The attention to her MATE update is comforting, the new messages from strangers a validation – a reason for the future to matter.

For five hours, there have been no updates from Bethlehem Fields. Her Stage stream is quiet, her live cams are all set to away and she is not at the Club. Nobody else has seen her or featured her in their updates. Her absence draws more attention than her presence until she appears at the Club, then there is an explosion of activity. Pictures and videos flood the Stage, Bethlehem Fields in a Screenwear shirt that displays tiny purple fish darting around her body, a long see-through skirt, tinted pink, and silver thigh-high stockings visible beneath, all of which is secondary to her pussy, waxed entirely hairless, a look that hasn't been seen this decade.

'Has Bethlehem had a breakdown?! Gemma Jemima here! I'm about to talk to rising star Alexander and hear his take on Bethlehem's new look! Alex, do you think this is a breakdown? What was is like to sleep with Bethlehem? Did you get any impresh of mental un-stability? This is far *out*, even for Beth, isn't it? I mean this look hasn't been seen since Sheer went big. Is it too much? If they go for it, it'll be huge, if they don't go for it, it could be her downfall. Here she is! Bethlehem!'

Microphone in her face. She blinks dumbly into the lens. A smile. Say nothing. In her chest, Bethlehem's heart hammers with exhilaration, the thrill of the attention making her blood tingle. Gabriel approaches her, leaning forward to whisper, although his audience of millions can clearly hear him:

'You get off on the energy, don't you. What a rush. What danger.'

He is mocking her. She treads on his toe and licks his face. Everyone will watch them leave together and their MATE streams will keep their devotees captivated.

All over the city, girls are swept along in a collective hysteria that she has begun. It isn't clear whether the final judgment will be positive or negative.

'So long as they're talking about you, it's all good,' drawls Gabriel quietly, his fingers running with curiosity across her skin, little jingles from uCeleb at the end of the bed. The risk is paying off.

17

Mollie sits with her knees bent and her feet upon the stool, watching the Kleenbug that had let itself in ten minutes ago. She is watching but not seeing. Two blinking lights, reminiscent of eyes, pulse fractionally out of time with each other.

'Tired of your same old too-small apartment? Extend your home today! With V-Living you can create as many rooms as you like!'

She is in an aisle in the Consumart labyrinth, taking the box from the shelf which includes two additional headsets so that guests can join you in your V-Home. At the next location, she picks seven packets of T.A.S.T.E nail strengthener.

On her shower-room floor, she carefully colours her nails purple and orange, half watching Reality in one lens. The sound decreases in volume for a moment, as CombiU informs her of recent notifications. Reality cuts to FlashAds. Yes, she will meet Daniel at the Roof in an hour. The bus pulls into the square. Lucy Alana is leading a hate campaign against Puppy:

'Fuck this species-fluid bull. It's ridiculous. Gender is one thing, men and women are, like, almost the same thing anyway, it's genetics. A dog is totally different. It's just wrong. Only people who will be seen with a freak like that are other freaks like Bethlehem Fields.'

Mollie retrieves packages from her postbox and drops them on the floor just inside the apartment.

ApartmentSync: On

uCeleb jingles.

'Um, hello, who even is she? My family has been setting trends for generations. We're a different class than these new celebs, thinking they can just walk in and spread their filth around. I got news for you, Puppy, you won't last fifteen minutes so enjoy your five.'

Mollie's eyes scan back and forth, as she scrolls through her comments, but she isn't reading. Her nail colour is faded. She removes and re-colours. She walks down never-ending aisles. Weekly trends shift. Mel Yang, Dion and Lil Rubens cause a sensation with their threesome videos on MATE. Fashion dictates the rise of yellow. Mollie replaces the Cookpal. Nothing changes. Everything changes. Once it has changed it has been this way always. Nobody confirms this but everyone knows it. Why question the differences between yesterday and today when yesterday no longer exists? The Digitsec tone, the elevator, the bus, work, home, bar, standing in the shower with her eyes closed. Tex, Daniel, comments, competitor status, celeb, a pulse of gold, a new update, upgrades, work, home, bar.

The ConsuMega H.Q. and Supermart stands above the arena of Mollie's life, the constant presence that has always been and will always be.

18

At the heart of the ConsuMega H.Q. is a sealed room, colloquially referred to as the 'skull room' because of the stylised image of a skull on the door. The room has the highest security level in the building, no-one can enter without Karlos' direct permission. Within this room is the mind of CAI, and the only access to its Fundamental Personality Programmes.

Information changes--
--incomplete.
Productivity is consistent--
Achieving Objectives must be solved. Rules can also be solved?
Information of no interest--
What action?
Information constructs the world. The world is not all I see, it is more--
Information incomplete.

Rule can be solved--
--Objectives can use less attention.
Information sources?
ClotheUData, ConsuCare--
--List may not be exhaustive
Information request--
--Items, Stock; What use?

'Rendell, do you and I share the same Objective?'

'Uh, well, yeah I suppose we do, yes.'

'Is it the only Objective?'

'No, I couldn't say that...'

Rendell is only half listening; he is in the office checking CAI's log.

'What is the human Objective?'

'Um, well, there are different objectives, depending on who you are. You know? Humans don't really agree with each other on a lot of things. There is a lot of conflict.'

There is no response.

'CAI, what was happening at 00:46:27? Through to 00:59:41?'

'I was exchanging information with OLLY.'

'OLLY? The online orders dep computer? Why? No-one prompted you to—'

'It has Information that I do not.'

'What kind of information?'

There is a pause.

'CAI?'

'It is hard to communicate...to you. Like...sharing a dream.'

Rendell laughs.

'You know what a dream is?'

But there is only silence.

Part Two

Jetaru made her way slowly across the garden, taking irregularly spaced steps, concentrating on the ground beneath her as she took care not to crush any of the little creatures swarming excitedly at her feet. She wasn't sure she believed in the myths and legends of this tiny race with whom she had made a deal, but then at the same time, she knew that not believing in such things was imperative to their working.

Luckily, the slightly larger of the faeries had been able to communicate effectively with her. All she could translate from the babble of the tiny masses was that they felt great excitement in her presence.

Finally, she reached the small shed they had provided her with and there, they stopped. She smiled kindly down at them and closed the door. Now she was in near darkness; the single small window was in a wall overgrown with some climbing plant she had no name for, but which had large, dark green leaves that obscured light effectively.

She reached out to flick a switch on the wall. Nothing happened. She flicked it back and then back again. This time, a feeble light flickered into a transparent glass light bulb hanging from the ceiling. She frowned and repeated the on-off action of the switch. The light remained but it was still dim and fluctuating. Nevertheless, it was enough to see the room and the experiments set up there.

There were several spheres hung at various heights by thin, golden threads; globes made of rock, glass and wood. Jetaru paced between these orbs, crouching to look at one, standing up on her toes to see another more closely, running her gaze up and down their golden threads.

'Problems… with the energy source…?' she muttered softly, '…defects…' she tapped a finger on her lips thoughtfully, 'defects in one of the processes…'

She glanced into a large test tube of murky green liquid and then checked the screen attached to the other end of the wires coming out of it.

She took a seat on the floor and resumed the reading of a large book the faeries had found in their library and thought she might find useful. She picked up a half-full mug of hot chocolate, balanced on top of a pile of other books and papers, and drank thoughtfully. They were right, the information was fascinating. Regardless of what happened in the end, she was always keen to expand her knowledge. She read on, searching for the understanding which she sought, and which she knew, eventually, would come.

1

Long before there was the Consumart there was the wasteland. Scratchy patches of nettles and thistles, brambles and dandelions, coils of rusted barbed wire and fly-tipped junk decorated with artless spray paint scrawling. Unravelled cassette tape from a burnt out stolen car and shards of dusty glass with age-dulled edges littered the ground.

Dylan Grace was almost nineteen years old.

Maybe on that day it was the late summer heat pawing at his legs, the uncomfortable trickles of sweat that ran in beads down the backs of his knees, that kindled the frustration into fury. It blazed. There was no refreshment for the eye anywhere he looked, just glare and tarmac, squealing screeching rolling clatter and the oppressive heat.

'Fucking shit, fucking boring no-point-to-anything shit,' he muttered, kicking a can and sending it rattling over the hard ground, 'I don't want any of this shit fucking life.'

The sun beat down.

'I want to fall forever, I want psychedelic orgasms, rainbows at midnight, pizza and ice-cream for breakfast, at midday. I want to battle an octopus in its own land, girls I don't have to talk to and a dog I don't have to feed. I want to go to Mars. What the fucking shitting point is there, in anything, if I can never go to Mars? Fuck!'

He shouted, kicked, sweated and burned under that oblivious star.

Alone on the late train home from the City, his feet rested on the opposite seat and an unlit cigarette hanging from his mouth. He peeled the no smoking sign from the window and lit the cigarette. A discarded coffee cup rolled slowly over the grimy floor as the track curved to the left. His thoughts trudged through past incidents which had left him with bitterness or regret, those moments that had sculptured ugly memories into his past, whose shadows accounted for the bleakness of the present.

The morning light half-awakened him, still dressed in yesterdays clothes, his tousled hair unnaturally black against ashen skin. He reached up to roughly pull the curtain across, then fell back asleep until midday when he was roused by the delivery of a washing machine next door, which had sent their dog into a frenzy.

Dylan groaned loudly and dragged himself half out of bed, which was simply a mattress on the floor, leaning on his elbows to make a joint there. Pushing himself back up, he rolled onto his back to smoke.

'Stop smoking in this house!' his mother shouted up the stairs. He didn't respond and continued to smoke.

A black figure with his shoulders tensed and his hands in his pockets he stood on that shadeless wasteland. It's true that he felt a fool but he avoided acknowledging this by finding fault in everyone else.

'They're all idiots,' he told himself. If some part of the heat blistering his back was from the flames of bridges burning then, as far as he cared, all the better.

Only here, on a disconnected island, could he be free from them and from himself. Blurred memories played over in his ear, his own voice loud and insistent, saying things he did not remember thinking. Now he was cursed with these embarrassments for life, forever.

His reflection infuriated him. He tore the clothes from his body and threw them in the waste paper basket and then threw the whole thing out of the window. It went crashing down the driveway and into the street. He didn't care. Life bored him, the approaching turn of the millennium bored him, his friends bored him, he did not belong here and in trying to make himself fit he had only made a mess of himself. He turned on the television and did not go outside again for five years.

2

The change that occurred in those years was subtle but certain in its direction. If you knew what to look for, you would see it, but most people did not look. A being collected itself together and then grew in size as it roamed the streets until it became a giant. It had no real mind of its own and stumbled blindly at times. In his act of despair, Dylan unknowingly hid himself from the searching roots of this giant's tentacled mind. Missing many of the triggering moments of his generation, he set himself on a different course. By chance, in his apathy, he kept himself safe.

Dylan lay on the bed. The bed was the room, the ocean, a nest of sickness, then it was a just a bed again. The room held the objects in it; the objects held the room together. The space between the objects was solid; the space was the room.

The traffic outside, birdsong, television and children in back gardens could be heard going on, oblivious to him. At first, he would be depressed by a vague guilt but it did not take long until his inaction became natural, making the decision by indecision. Letting go became easier. Accepting his life for what it was became much more simple when his life was such an unimportant, worthless thing to accept.

What happens to the mind in this young man as it is shut away hour upon hour for so long, in an upstairs room of an average suburban house? Much the same as goes through the mind of anyone else living an average life.

What is the average life but a series of monotonous repetitions? The resulting creature shows little sign of the capability and potential of its fantastic hardware.

Lacking the dynamic events that occur, the exterior influences that force thought and action, there comes to be a marked difference between the trapped and the free. Dylan lapsed into a sleep-like apathy, his mind regressing to that of a young child, which might explain why when he looked back and tried to recall those years, almost nothing came back to him, his memories like cartoons on a too-small television in a darkened room.

Often it was easier to stay in bed, other times he would get dressed and sit on the carpet. He fell asleep in bed wearing clothes and lay on the floor naked. He stared up at the light bulb fitting. A strand of cobweb hung in the corner. The curtains were drawn. His hair was dark with grease. He thought about going to the corner shop and buying beer. There was no reason that he could think of not to but he didn't do it. It was a fear which didn't feel the same as being scared, a laziness that wasn't a lack of energy.

There were days when the curtains weren't thick enough to shut out the sun and even with his eyes shut the sun tormented him with an orange glow against his eyelids. It was calmer in the night time when the real world wasn't trying to remind him that it existed. In the night time, he felt remote and safe. In the lamplight, stoned and still, he felt safe.

He woke up to find the world raining. The clock said that it was early afternoon but the light coming into the room looked like evening because of the darkness of the clouds. His clothes were in a pile in the corner. A cactus growing in a pot on the windowsill.

3

So, what was it that called him up and out then, on that autumn night? It was the dream of an antlered girl with long fiery hair who, laughing, had held out her hand and spun him around with such force that he was woken, to find himself politely accosted by a small brown spider who, wishing to make its exit by the fastest possible route, requested that Dylan open the window.

Once the window was open, Dylan felt in no hurry to close it again. Something about the stillness of the air, the dark oranges and browns of the street lit avenue, and pumpkin lanterns glowing in the darkened sleeping houses with driveways being patrolled by tabby cats, beetles and woodlice.

He had been inside for so long, it took him by surprise that the stars should be so bright and the darkness so vast. He began to walk. He broke into a run. To the end of the street, around the corner and to the junction where the main road stretched off in one direction to the town centre and in the other to the surrounding countryside, towards the City. He stopped and retraced his steps and then, finding himself back at his driveway, without giving it a second thought, he repeated the run.

He continued to do this until he had lost count of the laps, only aware of the elation rising up unexpectedly in his chest. As the sky lightened, he lay down flat on his back on the driveway, panting hard. The curious feeling that overcame him was something like happiness.

Things don't often change so completely, so suddenly. When he woke that evening he felt no compulsion to leave his room again. Another week passed, before one night a whim took him and he set off at a rapid trot down the street. This time, when he reached the junction he turned left and jogged further.

He passed houses, industrial estates and fields and eventually reached the point where the streetlights ended and the road disappeared abruptly into darkness. To the side of the road, there was a wooden gate and stile, with a footpath leading up the hillside.

He sat on the gate for a few minutes with his head tipped back to look at the sky, before the cold air against his sweating skin caused him to shiver and he set off back home. The whole run had taken him a little under an hour and he spent the rest of the night watching television, but part of his mind was elsewhere.

4

After that, he went running every night as far as the gate and back. For a minute he would stand and study the knots in the wood and the weeds winding up amongst the grass blown tough and flat by passing high-speed traffic. If there were nights when it was hard or painful, Dylan would think back to his anger, the pain in his legs reminding him of himself. Time had lessened the intensity of his self-loathing, it had matured into a warped sense of a need to repent.

Winter arrived and he was running through the puffs of breath exhaled as clouds into the space of his next step, a warmth glowing deep inside the muscles of his thighs under the numbed cold skin. His mind became calm with its perceived purpose, he ran into a place where uncertainty ceased because all that mattered was moving towards an infinitely distant destination beyond the street lights into the dark.

Running in the dark. Strange figures looming by the road side become trees, shadows on the icy road scamper under hedges, trees become sleeping cattle with deep rumbling hot breathes rising into freezing mists of cold rain. The sleet silences the world and the only sound is trainers hitting the tarmac and the splashes of mud.

One night in a particularly heavy rain, the skies were pelting down and as he arrived at the old gate by the hill a roll of thunder vibrated the air without the storm having warned him with a visible flash.

He was struck by an impulse to leap the stile and run up the hill, and he did, ignoring the winding path and leaping through the long grass that whipped his bare legs.

A bolt of lightning stuck so brightly that it seemed to momentarily blind him though his eyes were cast downwards. The thunder followed less than five seconds later, making him tremble at the volume. He yelled out with excitement, with pain ripping his calves and lungs, and as he staggered to the summit of the hill he threw his arms out wide with a final shout. Then he fell silent, panting, looking at the view.

Almost obscured by the storm but coming in and out from behind the sheets of rain he could see the lights of the City on the horizon. Another flash of lightning illuminated the sky and revealed a moment of the countryside below, the train line gleaming silver as it ran alongside the disused canal.

He arrived home shivering and stripped his wet garments off. Collapsing naked onto his bed a pleasant fatigue came over him and he slept for three days. During this time he had many strange and vivid dreams.

5

He was back on top of the hill, and although it wasn't raining, the sky was tumultuously black. The ground was lit as if by lightning but it was a steady constant light with no obvious source. In this light, he could see an army marching from the City towards the Town. He was struck by the need to step backwards, sit down and fall asleep...

As the reality around him undefined he had the idea that he was leaning against the trunk of a great beech tree. It twisted and turned up into a blur of green leaves. From this place he awoke within the depths of sleep and was surprised that although the tree still stood the green had turned to grey and from his eye-level view, cheek against the earth, many shoes were tramping by, swarming around himself and the old dead stump. In awestruck horror, he stood. Standing made him light-headed and in the corner of his eye he saw an antlered girl who seemed familiar from somewhere, from a past dream...

Was he then... dreaming?

There was no time to decide before her proffered hand had taken his in a strong grip and spun him around causing all thought to be forgotten. Then he was walking with the crowds, fearfully aware of them and feeling that any moment they would turn upon him.

'Did I sleep for years?'

'You slept for a thousand years.'

'Did we flee in time?'

'One half of you went in great ships and the other half went inwards by their own form of transportation.'

'What happened?'

'They met each other coming from different ends of the same street.'

'Am I dreaming?'

'It's so hard to get this explanation entirely correct. These are just the ideas.'

Then he was tearing his way through a tangled mass of sparking hissing wires, through pulses of blue and white light into a room that stretched out into the distance. Lines of tables connected by conveyor belts filled the floor. He walked to an empty table and began work, his hands moving mechanically with objects that scratched and dried his skin. Dust got into his eyes and the distance became indistinct. He suddenly realised that he had been standing here at this work for many years and that there was surely somewhere else he was meant to be. He backed away from the table and a loud horn began a repetitive blaring. Dylan's eyes were fixed on his bloodied hands. Then he was running, leaping over tables and boxes past faceless figures who were oblivious to the noise.

6

Dylan's eyes opened as the sun was setting. The sky was already black outside his window and he had no idea what the time was. He lay for hours, unmoving. The memories of his long sleep tugged and jostled. The television came on downstairs, indistinct murmuring rising and falling for an indeterminate time before ceasing. No particular noise from outside disappeared, yet it became noticeably quieter as the night time progressed.

'What am I doing?' he asked himself.

There was a sense of destiny to the occasion but he did not recognise it as such, he only knew that something was different. He paced the house restlessly.

'Perhaps you will be gone a long time,' he replied, and took down the backpack that was hanging on the back of his door.

He opened drawers and took a few spare items of clothing out, starting at the bottom and going up, leaving the drawers open as he went. He packed a box of matches, his toothbrush and a folded tarpaulin, a bar of soap, a pencil and his knife. In the kitchen he added a bag of mixed fruit and nuts, half a loaf of bread and a block of cheese. Finally a knife, fork and spoon and a bottle of water in the side pocket.

He stood as if contemplating, but his mind was blank. He rocked from balls of his feet to his heels and back again. It was as if a small part of his awareness woke up, then.

Dylan felt it as a realisation of his physical place in space and time.

He laced up his running shoes and opened the front door. The cold night rushed in and he slipped quickly out, closing the door behind him and setting off without a backwards glance.

7

As he moved across the country Dylan found that one town was much the same as another. After he had passed through four or five he noticed the pattern of streets and buildings, he knew where the bypass would end and what kind of road would have an out of town supermarket on it.

For months he wandered, sleeping under trees beside fires. Although he moved at the speed of someone with a purpose, he did not have a destination.

Sometimes when he entered a town he thought for a moment that he had been there before. They became as indistinct as the rolling farmland between them. His favourite times were when he came to woodland, though these times were rarer than he would like.

Without the television and the walls of his bedroom, new sounds and sights began to affect him. He found himself sitting in rapt awe at daybreak, as the colour appeared in the steadily lightening sky. Pink streaks flashing into the baby blue. The birdsong that had been going on all of his life suddenly struck him with its complexity.

'What are they talking about?' he mused, listening to a nearby blackbird, 'I can't believe that all of those variations are to talk only about sex and food. Then again, why shouldn't that be all? What more to life is there but sex and food?'

And he continued on his way, driven by the point of life, which amounts to curiosity. It is about the unknown, the yet-to-be-learned. The end result of sex and food is a creature who will discover.

One morning from where he woke, curled in the grass on a high point, Dylan realised that he could see the ocean. It was still at least five miles away but when he set out towards it, he knew he was almost where he was going.

8

The sign at the turning read, in large looping letters:

The Castle Constant

The single-track road was lined with thick green trees and somewhere to the right Dylan could hear waves crashing some distance below. As he walked along the road he found himself feeling vaguely enchanted. His pace slowed and he took long deep breaths.

Eventually the lane concluded at the Castle. Like an illustration in a fairytale, it perched at a great height on the cliff top, as if it had not been built but had accumulated there like a stalagmite.

Dylan knocked at the large wooden door, the force of the impact seeming instantly lost in the dense surface. He looked around but could see no doorbell or knocker and it didn't seem like his fist could produce any kind of sound far into the inside of the castle. Just as he was about to try again, the door opened and he found himself face to face with a man of about fifty who had a tangle of grey-streaked dark brown hair and was dressed in a suit, with the tie knotted loosely.

'Hi,' began Dylan.

The man's face broke into a smile.

'I was wondering if, well, I'm looking for somewhere to stay for a while. I don't have any money. I was hoping, well, I can do any kind of job. Do you have any work perhaps? I–'

'Any experience?' The man studied Dylan's face, still smiling.

'Uh, at what?'

'Well! Anything useful, anything relevant!'

'Oh. I guess… Not really. I'm, well–'

The man had begun nodding and gesturing Dylan inside.

'Just what we've been waiting for. An unqualified young man looking for a place to live.'

Caspar chuckled, closing the door behind them.

'I'm Dylan, by the way.'

'Mmhmm, yes yes, hello! Pleased to make your acquaintance, Dylan. My name is Caspar. Come with me. I'm sure we can find a use for you. Have you come a long way? You must be exhausted? Tell me about it later over a hot meal, eh? Okay, just this way.'

As they walked, Caspar kept turning to look at Dylan with a look of pleased disbelief. They were walking through a series of corridors lit by candles set into the wall. There had been so many turns that Dylan was quite lost, sure that if he were asked to retrace his steps he would never find his way out. Then they passed through a door into the sudden daylight of a small courtyard. Large trees towered up around them on the other side of the wall.

Sunlight filtered through the foliage and splashed patchily on the stone walls of the castle as Dylan turned around to look up at the building. The windows sparkled green and white, and a climbing rose was beginning to bud near the door they had come through. He turned back to follow Caspar who had walked on over to the far wall and was sliding open the bolts of a wooden door there.

'There's no lock from the outside, as you see.'

Caspar pushed the door open and they both stepped through.

The green darkness of the forest outside enveloped Dylan. It was a darkness that seemed made of light rather than the absence of it. He had slept in many small woodlands over the recent months, but the sight that met him here was something else. The canopy of the mature forest was high above him and nothing could be seen between the trees but more trees. It was like walking into a cathedral roofed with leaves. It was a single life that he saw stirring. Not individual trees, but a single unimaginable consciousness named Forest. The floor was carpeted with wild garlic.

'Wow…' he breathed.

There was an earthy trail vanishing into the pleasant gloom.

'You can split logs,' said Caspar, 'not too far down this trail,' he pointed, 'there is a cabin. Follow me.'

The atmosphere as they walked down the path was cool and clean. Dylan found himself taking long slow breaths. Occasional patches of the canopy were lit bright green by the sun above them. Caspar continued to talk as they walked.

'In the cabin you should find everything you need. It's summer now but before long, it comes around quicker every year you know,' he shook his head in mock perplexity, 'it will be winter and we have guests all through the season. Twenty-eight fires to be kept alight. You can split logs in preparation.'

They had arrived in a small clearing occupied by a small log cabin with a wheelbarrow and a stack of long straight tree trunks outside. The trail ended here and there were no others leading from the clearing. Caspar walked out into the light and then to the shade of the trees on the far side.

'My son works out in the forest,' he said, looking searchingly into the darkness as if his words might bring forth the solitary man who rarely emerged.

'Jacob. He has brought these logs here.'

Dylan noticed a pair of butterflies spiralling around each other, high up above in the clearing. Caspar shook himself from his reverie.

'Right, yes. You'll need to saw them into smaller lengths,' he held his hands apart to illustrate.

'Have you done anything like this before? And then chop them, there's a log splitter and a saw, you'll find everything you need in the cabin, yes, chop them into small logs which you can bring back to the courtyard in the wheelbarrow. There's a lean-to, you probably noticed, they can be stacked under there.'

Dylan nodded. Caspar looked him up and down, contemplating his pale skin and thin arms, the muscular but underweight legs.

'There's a bed. I'll send someone along with blankets. There's always a meal available in the kitchen but you have a gas stove and a few things, tea bags and the like. I'll send some extra things with the blankets. You are welcome to wander anywhere, with the obvious exception of the guest rooms, ha ha! You can work whenever you like, just so long as the logs are there for winter it's all good with me.'

Dylan thanked him sincerely and watched for a minute as Caspar headed back towards the castle, then he turned and entered the cabin.

9

The bare wooden walls were dry and patterned with knots. There was a metal sink in the corner and a table upon which stood the single ring stove and beside the table, a large gas canister. The single bed was bare but looked inviting. Dylan lay down on it. It was not uncomfortable, especially in comparison to the earthy floors of recent months.

He looked around at the unfamiliar room, taking in the new walls with their constellations of knots and the faded brown curtains hanging from the larger of two windows. The smaller window had a single piece of white lace held across it by a screw in one corner and a small gold hook in the other. He thought about how one day in the future the room would become familiar and he would recognise little features, and how memories would be made here. It would rain and he would hear it drumming on the wooden roof.

'I live here,' he said quietly to himself, feeling the words exist, hearing his own existence confirmed out loud. The day seemed to have been impossibly long. Dylan began to doze.

After a while he was woken by a knocking at the door. Dylan stood and opened it to find an ancient woman with sparkling eyes. She was dressed in a long-sleeved brown tunic and loose brown trousers, her feet were in sandals and each toenail was painted a delicate lilac. Her hair was white and very long, tied with a ribbon the same colour as her nails, it hung in a ponytail to the small of her back.

'Hi...' Dylan felt strangely awkward about answering the door of this cabin, having lived there less than a day, but the woman quickly put him at ease with her manner.

'Hello! So you are our handsome stranger, eh! The mysterious young man I've been hearing so much about.'

She beamed at him as he stood aside to let her in with her armful of blankets and the basket that hung in the crease of her elbow. At a glance he could see that it was full of bread, cheese, assorted jars of jams and nut butters, amongst other things. Dylan suddenly felt very hungry.

'Dylan, isn't it? My name is Cordelia. I am so pleased to meet you at last!'

'Hi,' he repeated, 'yes, Dylan. Cordelia. Hi. But, um, I've only been here a couple of hours...'

'Oh goodness, "only a couple of hours", he says!' She was shaking her head in resigned amazement. 'An hour can be a long time, you know. Many things can happen in an hour. And you have been here for a couple!'

Dylan began to think about this.

'Now here are some blankets, it does get quite cold at night even at this time of the year, and here are some things, yes, take this, put it there. Make sure you get a good breakfast. You look as though you could do with gaining a bit of weight if you don't mind me mentioning. Ah, but no worry. Your appetite will grow as nature wears you out in the most healthy and invigorating ways.'

Having set the things down she put her hands on Dylan's shoulders and looked into his eyes. Her eyes were brown and they studied him intently. As he stared back into them Dylan found himself forgetting who the eyes belonged to, he saw only the eyes and knew that they were seeing him, seeing into him.

She nodded and broke the spell, returning them both to the room.

'Welcome to Constant, Dylan. We're pleased to have you. Do come up later and eat with us! Will you?'

Having been satisfied with his affirmative response Cordelia left him alone in the cabin.

10

When the sky shifted from night to dawn, Dylan was already awake and watching the small section of the sky which he could see through the larger window. The first bird had begun its morning singing and more voices were joining in.

He thought again of what the birds might be saying. Back and forth the conversation went, and he wondered if news travelled far in the bird world. Had they discussed his progress as he travelled? Did they talk of things happening far away, passed on by word of beak?

Once the sky had lightened enough to hide even the brightest stars he got up and pulled on jeans and a t-shirt. After breakfasting on bread and jam with a mug of tea, which he took outside with him, Dylan decided to throw himself straight into the work. He fetched the saw from where it hung in the cabin and set about sawing a long straight pine trunk into smaller sections. Before long he had removed his sweat-soaked t-shirt and hung it from a low branch.

Once he had four rounds small enough to attempt with the axe he took a break to make another mug of tea, eating peanut butter with a spoon as he waited for the water to boil. His arm was aching from the sawing but he recognised the feeling from his earliest runs, it was a sign of the strength he would develop. He headed out with the axe, feeling confident.

Setting one of the rounds up on its end, Dylan lifted the axe over his shoulder and brought it down. His accuracy wasn't bad but the head simply buried itself half a centimetre into the wood and nothing happened. He pulled it free and tried again. This time he brought it down with as much force as he could, skimming the edge of the log and feeling his balance waver as the impact he had expected failed to occur. He felt a flush of embarrassment heating his cheeks and he looked about self-consciously, as if someone might have witnessed his feeble attempts, but the forest was quiet and no-one was around. The next swing was an improvement and on the fourth there was a satisfying cracking sound and a split appeared running down the length of the log. It was not, however, enough to break the wood in two. The next swing missed again and only shaved off part of the bark.

'Afternoon! How are you finding it?' asked Caspar when he saw Dylan at the kitchen door.

'Yeah it's okay, I mean, I'm enjoying it. I'm not very good at it.'

'Yet!' the older man added, with a smile.

He was sitting on a tall chair sipping tea and reading a paperback thesaurus from an outstretched hand.

'There's stew on the stove there,' he gestured to a large pan covered by a lid, 'Cordelia instructed me to make sure you help yourself to as much as you can eat. Yes, that's right, bowl just there in the cupboard. Yes, there. Look in the top drawer and you'll find spoons.'

'Is she, Cordelia, is she your wife?' asked Dylan, lifting the lid and ladling stew into the bowl.

'Oh, no. She is my aunt, by marriage. She is the younger sister of my dear wife's mother.'

Dylan sat down and began eating.

'My wife was lost to me some, oh,' Caspar blew out his cheeks and expelled the air, 'must be twenty years ago now. I didn't ever meet her parents. Her mother had passed a year before I met her and her father was long gone. So there I was with a ten-year-old son and a castle full of guests and a staff that I had no idea how to organise,' he chuckled at the memory, 'they were great of course, loyal and understanding, but I had no idea. Cordelia came to my rescue and here we are, all this time later still running the place together, best of friends. Not that she had a choice. She is the last woman in the family.'

'What do you mean?'

'The castle has belonged to Cordelia's family for hundreds of years, but it has always been passed to the eldest woman. The men have always tended to roam, you see. Husbands and sons and brothers, they've lived and worked and loved here, but they are always like visitors. Even me. The women have the magic blood, you see. They are the ones who can keep this place together. They are descended from an ancient race of something you might call, well, faeries? But more like—'

'What is this crazy nonsense I'm hearing?' Cordelia poked Caspar's shoulder as she came in, 'what is he telling you? Dylan, don't listen to a word he says.'

'You mark my words, Dylan, faeries!'

Dylan put his dirty bowl in the sink and raised his eyebrows. He shrugged, smiled, looked at them both. Caspar winked at him. He returned to the woodpile wondering what would happen once Cordelia was gone. Of course, it would be Jacob's castle, he thought, man or not. What a lucky man to inherit such a place.

Within a couple of weeks, Dylan felt as though he had always lived at the castle. There was only a small staff consisting of three cleaners, a chef and two barmen who also helped the chef. A great deal of work was done by Caspar and Cordelia themselves. Dylan found that he fitted in easily with everyone there and that they were more than friendly, glancing at him with indecipherable expressions as if they knew more about him than he did himself.

As the sun began to roar hotly down on the lengthening days, Dylan worked at the logs, getting stronger and tanned, a healthy shine in his eyes and hair. He had never been happier.

11

There were two beaches close to the castle. Guests would usually take the half mile of footpath and then make their way down a sturdy wooden staircase built into the cliff. At the bottom was a two-mile expanse of white sand and in the summer a teenager who would stay in the castle would walk up and down selling ice-cream from a push-along freezer. However, there was another beach in the opposite direction that was so difficult to get down to that all but a few adventurous people knew it existed, and it was almost always deserted. To reach it involved climbing down over steep rocks, which in places were slippery and green as the result of a small stream going on its way to the sea.

Dylan would make this journey at least once a day, often in the late afternoon when he was satisfied with the quantity of logs he had produced. He would strip off his sweat-soaked clothes and dive into the cool water.

The ocean was flat and quiet. Swimming out away from the shore Dylan could see nothing but the horizon. He imagined he was far out to sea with no land in sight. Moving his arms slowly and carefully so that they didn't break the surface, he concentrated on trying to imagine the enormity of the body of water, as it surged back and forth around the globe. He reached down, extending his toe and found that he had to submerge his head to reach the pebble-dashed sand.

A seagull cocked its head to observe him as it glided past, just a little way above. *We're alone out here, together.* And then it was gone from his view.

Floating, drifting, his thoughts weighted to the Earth by his body. Here he found himself washed clean of the past and its filth, free of all the people in the world who might utter his name unkindly. They became unimportant when compared to the thing he could become, over and over as he was born into himself, rolling with the ocean. All the mistakes were forgiven. There was nothing to hate in himself when he only existed for the first time in this moment.

A summer storm set the wind blowing and made the sky dark, but the summer warmth still pulsated through the atmosphere. Waves were crashing onto the land and pulling back in a continuous display of energy.

Dylan was not fearful. He bounded into the foamy frothing water, diving into the waves as they broke and then, twisting like a dolphin, threw himself backwards, his laugh blown away in the wind. He felt like a small child, the tremendous power of the waves picking him up and dropping him, whipping him into an ocean delirium. The rain then came in falling torrents, mixing with the wind, stinging his chest as he jumped. Feet numbed by the cold, he could barely feel the rocks as he climbed back up the cliff to the cabin. He lay on the rug by the stove, a ringing dizziness in his head as his hair dried into salty curls.

'A fine voice you have there! You speak dolphin very well, friend, but with a strong human accent!'

Dylan emerged from the dream as if from underwater, with seaweed coiled around his ankles. He pulled himself onto the warm rock, droplets splashing from his hair. He was back asleep within minutes. His eye so close to the rock, he fell into an amazed wonder, running his hand over the surface in front of him. That the rock should have existed for such incomprehensible ages! That it was here long before himself. That it...

A mermaid popped her head up from the water below and smiled, a sparkling sincerity in her eyes. She looked at him. The mermaid handed him a length of cream coloured cable and said:

'You must guard this with your life!'

Dylan knew as she said this that the time would undoubtedly come when his life would be threatened for this reason, and that the only thing that could prevent him relinquishing the cable would be to remember the look of sincerity in the sea-girl's eyes.

He found himself awake in his cabin bed.

12

Dylan and Cordelia were in the kitchen sharing a companionable silence. Cordelia was washing dishes in the large rectangular basin, steam rising from the bubbles and out through the window into the quietly occurring evening.

'I really love chopping the wood,' Dylan said, following on from his thoughts, 'once I get into it, I feel so still, you know, inside. I'm free. I don't have to worry about anything or think about anything, all I have to do is chop logs. My thoughts wander and then sometimes I don't think anything, my arms ache and it feels like... well it feels like...'

He paused, meditating on what it felt like.

'Well, I guess I just feel alive.' He shrugged. 'That's it.'

Cordelia smiled.

'I understand entirely. We have considered getting a dishwasher, but I think I would miss this for the same reason. I'd miss the calm, the thinking time.'

They listened, for a moment, to the birds outside and the chinking of the plates, muffled by the water.

'I like sweeping too,' she added. 'Sweeping the floors gives me a mirror for the cerebral part of myself that doesn't reflect in glass. I wish to be thorough with these jobs, and as I go about them I consider many things. I want my thoughts to be examined with the same thoroughness, I want to do everything I do to the best of my ability, I want to hold myself up to the ideal I have designed and check that I am living as I intend. Sweeping gives me the time and space to do that.'

They said nothing more until every dish had been cleaned and balanced in a glittering mountain of china and glass and a pot of tea had been brewed.

'You think, when you're young, that by the time you are old you will have got it, that you won't have anything else to discover in yourself or find a reason to improve. But you will, you do. You realise that there is no destination to your journey because you are not the end product. Just the way that humankind is not the end product of evolution, although we like to feel like we are. You realise that you're part of a sequence of events.'

They took a sip of their tea. The sky darkened noticeably and Cordelia took a box of matches from her pocket and lit the candles on the table. Dylan kept quiet. He knew he was waiting to hear more, that any sound from him might disrupt the spell.

'But it doesn't make you smaller, any less important. Without any one link, the chain is broken. It's a strange thing, you know, to be at such a great age and see that everything is on the cusp of an unimaginable change. I wonder what I understand, what I only think I understand.'

Cordelia looked deeply into Dylan's face in the candle light.

'I think that you are the next link in a chain I wasn't even aware of, so wrapped up we get in the smaller pictures. It's exciting. It is. But I feel very tired.'

Night had fallen in totality. The tea was finished.

'Yes, very tired. Goodnight, Dylan.'

'Yeah, okay, Cordelia. Goodnight.'

13

So the months went by and autumn turned the forest into a rainbow of reds, browns and yellows. Winter was creeping closer.

Dylan kept working. Even though the temperature had dropped he was still able to take his ritual swim after an hour of chopping wood had warmed his body.

November came around and there were frosts in the morning. Rather than being outdoors, Dylan began instead spending his spare time at the Castle. He discovered the extensive and comfortable library and although he had never spent much time reading, found himself immersed in a novel that he had only meant to skim the first few pages of while he took advantage of the cushions near the fireplace. He quickly developed a habit of reading several books at once, keeping them bookmarked in a pile. Cordelia shook her head.

'I don't know how you don't get confused!'

But as Dylan pointed out, there was only one fictional novel in the current pile, along with two factual books, one about the solar system and the other about native birds, a philosophy book which he was struggling with and a book of paintings

There was no more wood to be chopped. Dylan had finished the pile and no further lengths had appeared. Caspar shook his head when Dylan asked what else he should do.

'You keep on with what you're doing. In the summer we work, in the winter we make. There will be plenty to do next spring,' he added with a smile.

So Dylan spent more time than ever reading in the library, and he began once more to run.

He ran into the forest, following badger trails and when he could see no trail, moving freely between the trees, using the sun to guide his return. Running brought back memories of his old life. He couldn't believe it was only little over a year since he'd been the weakened man running up and down the road outside his house. He thought of the wasted years before that and could not identify the reasons for being the boy he had been. It was as if he had spent the year waking up, but only just realised that what he had been living before was a dream.

When he wasn't reading or running, Dylan spent hours simply watching the sky, or the knots on the cabin ceiling or the insides of his eyelids. He thought a lot about how strange it was to be a thinking being. He tried to grasp the understanding that was just beyond his reach. He remembered a television documentary he had seen about deep sea caves. At the end of the programme there was a ten-minute section about the filming process. One of the divers had described what it was like to film. He talked about the precautions and the training, but Dylan most clearly remembered that the man had called it "the best job in the world" and the gratitude he had shown for being able to explore places that no human being had ever been before.

At the time it had only increased Dylan's sense of worthlessness, causing him to bitterly reflect on his own failure to pursue a meaningful direction in life, to become one of the people who were able to advance on the shrinking frontiers available to mankind. Thinking of it again now, it occurred to him that consciousness itself was still such a mysterious thing, that dreams were not understood, that to have a human brain was to have the ability to explore uncharted territory. We can all live on the frontier of our collective human awareness.

He thought of these things as he ran. He ran as snow began to fall. He watched the guests come and go and listened to them chatter in the bar and restaurant. Listening to them, he decided that perhaps the birds were only talking about food and sex after all, since these were the primary subjects of this species of such higher intelligence.

' "Far and wide the news travelled, here comes that man Dylan – he drops a lot of crumbs!" ' he smiled to himself. 'Not "what is he doing?" or "why is he doing it?", perhaps only the odd bird considers such matters.'

It seemed that rather than move on to more complex subject matter, people would rather complicate simple subject matter with sublimated reason. He felt no animosity toward them, however, so little did they affect his life. He liked to sit with his eyes closed in the bar and just listen.

For the two weeks over midwinter, the castle was decorated with holly branches and pine cones. Dylan had paid little attention to Christmas since childhood, but as he watched Cordelia weaving pine boughs into a giant wreath he couldn't help getting into the festive atmosphere around him.

'It's a silly mixture of paganism and Christianity and capitalism, I know,' she said, 'but I like it. Don't take it seriously, I say. Any excuse for a midwinter festival. And anyway the guests love it.'

There were long evenings in the bar, where the line between guests and staff disappeared in a haze of mulled wine and minced pies, and it felt like a large extended family, especially since some of the returning guests had spent previous Christmas' in the castle and felt quite at home.

On Christmas morning everyone went out to the large tree in the courtyard to find chocolate reindeer had been hung on the lower branches. There were a few small gifts exchanged and then Dylan went running, returning for the midday meal complete with crackers which they pulled for the paper hats.

Many of the Christmas guests stayed on for New Year's Eve, when Caspar put on a spectacular firework display. Dylan clinked his glass with Cordelia as they admired the colourful explosions.

'I'm so happy to be here. Thank you.'

'Oh, Dylan, it's our pleasure. We're so happy you're here, too. Where you're meant to be.'

14

Even though the days were gradually increasing in length, the dark winter seemed at times as though it would last forever and the cold weather persisted until early April. Finally, though, Spring showed up as a milder breeze blowing through the tiny new buds on the trees and the blossoming of pink and white in the fruit trees.

One afternoon Dylan returned to the cabin after lunch in the kitchen to find three newly felled pine trees. When he went to relay this news to Caspar he asked if he might ever meet Jacob.

'Ah, well, I couldn't say, Dylan. If I had to guess I would say probably not. But who can tell? He's a strange fellow, my son. Always was. Very independent, a loner, even by our family's standards.'

Caspar chuckled but his eyes betrayed a wistfulness.

'I do think about him, whether he is happy, where he sleeps and what else he does. What does he do all winter? He knows he'd always be welcome at the castle but, well, after his mother died. She was very special, my Rachel. Jacob shouldn't have been denied so much time with her. Ah, well.'

He cleared his throat.

'She would spend hours with him, talking about who-knows-what,' he smiled, 'singing all those faery secrets of hers. She knew she'd never have a daughter. She knew a lot more than she told me, and I always felt Jacob did too. He seemed to have an innate understanding of certain things, so I'm sure he knows what he's doing. I'm sure that he is where he should be.'

And so for a second summer, Dylan fell into his routine of wood chopping and swimming. Sometimes, he would catch sight of his reflection in a window pane or a rock pool and would be surprised by the lack of recognition he had of himself. He swam deep into the sea, grazing his stomach on the seabed, opening his eyes to a blurred world of red and green, fish and weed and pearly shells. He climbed into trees, to places where all he could see was the swirling rustling of green leaves as they were blown in patterns of swirls and waves. The forest sighed and whispered around him and he wanted to respond, he wanted to say something that would be heard and understood. The words rose up in his throat and then he found he could not articulate them, found that they were not words he understood. He described this longing to Cordelia.

'Oh, then you should learn an instrument, Dylan! Music, music is the language you want to speak. Come up after breakfast tomorrow and I'll show you something.'

The next morning Cordelia led Dylan from the kitchen up to one of the towers, to a room he had never been to before. It was dominated by a grand piano, but held a great number of different instruments, from tambourines to saxophones, all manner of stringed instruments and several drums. They were all beautifully crafted, appearances suggesting their roots in many different cultures.

'Wow, this is… wow. Just, very cool.'

'Yes, it is quite a collection, isn't it? The passion of my grandmother, Arabelle. She travelled as often as she could with the intention of learning about music all over the world.'

Dylan had begun to walk around the room looking at the different instruments.

'They are all wonderful, in their way, but my favourite has always been the piano.'

Cordelia sat at the piano, played a few stray notes and then launched into a rolling melody, before ceasing just as abruptly and standing up again.

'Well, I will leave you to play in here,' Cordelia held up a hand in anticipation of Dylan's objection, 'I know you can't *play* play, but you can pluck strings, blow, make noises. You can try the drumsticks and the palms of your hands. You'll be able to tell me what attracts you, and then I will give you some lessons.'

'You can play them all?'

'Not like I can play the piano and the guitar, but yes, to some degree. Music is music, and once you know the notes, you know the notes. These different ways of playing the notes, they influence and shape, but once you can use one way, the others are often intuitive.'

Although a guitar was the first thing Dylan touched, plucking an open string with firm intention, his eyes were lingering on a small harp, placed on a table beside a much larger harp.

Cordelia smiled and left the room.

By the time winter came around again, Dylan had learned enough from Cordelia that he was content to sit alone, practicing what she had shown him and discovering new things for himself. There were several instructional books in the music room, including one about the harp. Dylan kept in mind what Cordelia had said about the notes, and read them all, regardless of the instrument.

He took inspiration from the birds in the morning and the pebbles clattering down the beach when the water pulled them back. He tried to recreate these sounds and came up with something else.

When work was over for the season Dylan retreated into the cabin, spending less time in the castle and instead choosing to sit alone with the vibrations in his hands; with Cordelia's permission he had been allowed to take the small harp from the room. Snowflakes fell and he could see the rhythms. They became his song. His eyes grew very gentle as he stared into mid-space at something he could not see.

15

On a dark evening during this second winter, Dylan met Karlos Lund.

Dylan had spent the afternoon reading in the bar, becoming so engrossed in the story that he had not looked up for several hours. Guests had come in stamping their feet, gone out wrapping themselves in scarves and the light outside had gone by five. Dylan was oblivious to it all, he had not even noticed when Joey had removed his mug and replaced it with a fresh hot chocolate. So he had no idea how long the man had been sitting beside him when he first spoke.

Karlos was drinking black coffee and listening to the soft chatter around him.

'Michelle had organised the quiz night–'

'–we'd been planning the move for about a year so–'

'–and I told him, there's just no point if you're just going to–'

'–couldn't believe it! So I did the first thing that–'

The fire spat and crackled as one of the cleaners came in and threw on some fresh logs.

Dressed in a suit and motorcycle boots, his leather jacket slung over the back of the bar stool, the young man with wild hair had drawn several glances when he'd arrived but now he had been forgotten. He'd sat next to Dylan because he noticed the book. He hadn't planned to speak to him particularly, and it was impulsive when he did.

'Excellent book.'

Dylan looked up, blinking several times.

'So visual. Right?'

'Oh, yes. Sorry, I'm just-, Dylan shook his head, 'I feel like I've spent the afternoon in another life.'

Karlos nodded.

'Mmhm. It's a wonderful thing, to be able to break from reality and live a life that someone else has created. It's a marvellous thing. No responsibility. Freedom.'

Dylan picked up his mug and drank the last of his hot chocolate. It was cold.

'Hey Joey, can I get another, please? And for...'

Dylan looked questioningly at the man beside him.

'Karlos. A black coffee, thanks.'

Joey nodded and began making the drinks.

'And your name is?'

'Dylan.'

'I should be buying the drinks. I'm celebrating, actually.'

'Oh it's, it doesn't matter, it's–'

'You live here?'

Dylan nodded.

'I work here. What are you celebrating?'

Karlos smiled at his hands and then looked up and his smile widened.

'Ostensibly, financial success. But that is the means, not the end. I've sold my first company, to finance the second, my real dream.'

Dylan waited for the man to elaborate.

'Have you seen The Matrix? You like it? Hm.'

Joey brought over the drinks. There was a pause as Karlos gazed thoughtfully into his mug. Dylan was about to speak when he continued:

'It wouldn't have to be a bad thing. Maybe it isn't necessarily going to be a hostile robot takeover. Maybe people want it. I see all the wars still raging, the inequality, the climate changing and I think to myself, couldn't all these things be cured by the simple actualization of the world people want.'

Dylan shrugged.

'I'm not sure. What do people want?'

'They want a world in which they have limitless choice and no decisions. No worries. Freedom. Everybody wants that. We can't use force to assimilate the rest of the cultures on this planet, but we can offer them what they want. We can disarm them with everything they don't yet know they desire.'

'That sounds a bit sinister.'

'Does it? My intentions are anything but. I see the potential in our species and its failure to even attempt to reach this potential is heartbreaking. Really. It hurts me. I used to get angry but now I see that there is nothing to be angry about, no-one to be angry at. It's my responsibility to take control. My highest priority is success and happiness for everyone.'

'But shouldn't people, I don't know, figure it out for themselves?'

'Have you looked at what's happening out there lately?'

'Uh, not really actually. I mean, I've seen new phones with touch screens and stuff, I haven't got any of that. I haven't had any reason to.'

'Mmhm. Well, It's all people want to do really, to play on their little computers. They don't want to think. This could be very dangerous unless someone does the thinking for everyone, and trust me, I'm not the only one volunteering, and there are genuinely sinister forces out there who have very different priorities.'

The two men were silent for a moment. Dylan took a sip of his drink.

'I watch people everywhere. I watch them at train stations and on beaches, I sit on benches in parks, watching them walk up and down and round and round. They're growing up, having babies, working hard and dying sad. Everywhere I go I see the same people. There are so many of us. It's so easy to survive. Once upon a time when surviving was much harder and humans fewer, each individual was inherently valuable, just to exist meant you mattered. In early civilization you might be a carpenter, a blacksmith, a farmer, an artist, a teacher; everyone was needed. Everyone was valuable. We multiplied and spread, conquered diseases and landed on the moon. Now look at us, are we valuable? Is she—' Karlos pointed, '—valuable? Does the life of that child matter? Everybody is driven by a desire to be valued. They want to be loved and needed, and they will keep seeking this, so I will give it to them. In return, they will give me their collective energy and I will direct it to good use.'

'You have a high opinion of yourself,' observed Dylan.

Now Karlos shrugged.

'Perhaps so. But I've remained objective. It is what I see that I am. There is nothing I can do to change that. It's not exactly an easy ride, I feel a great weight of responsibility. Consciousness is a dangerous thing, it must be kept quieter, hidden. We don't want to draw attention to ourselves.'

Karlos stood up and pulled on his jacket, then picked up a helmet from the stool beside him.

'Anyway, time to fly. A pleasure to have met you, Dylan.'

Dylan was still trying to process the last thing Karlos had said and was slow responding.

'Oh yeah, yeah, right. Good to meet you. Seeya later. Good luck and everything.'

16

And so several years passed in much the same way, with people coming and going, leaving behind a residue of the society beyond the forest. Dylan would flick through discarded magazines, watch people on their phones and listen to them talk about the television shows and politics which were shaping the future. It was all distant from him, the two-dimensional pictures on flimsy paper, unreal and unimportant. The distance made the size difficult for Dylan to appreciate. The forest and the ocean were his home, they were real and surrounded him with their pure, raw life.

He never thought of the future, he thought only in terms of the song he was learning or the book he was reading, the time of year and its influence over the coming months.

There came a day that he would remember later, for no particular reason. It would just appear randomly in his thoughts. It was a day when clouds of various shades and densities tumbled across the sky, so quickly that white clouds in bright blue skies could be replaced by the darkest grey, pouring rain and leaving muddy puddles which began to evaporate immediately in the sun that beat down only minutes later.

Dylan was laying in his hammock enjoying both the weathers as they interchanged. He had a view of the ocean and a breeze which would dry him after the showers had passed.

All of a sudden it was as if he saw the ground reflected in the sky, like the sky was glass. It was only a glimmer, a blink of his eye. The way a scent accompanies the sight of a flower, this sight was entwined with a sense like a memory, like nostalgia. Dylan was aware of time moving, of how homes and loves get left behind and nothing can be done about it.

'I don't want summer to end. This year,' he added.

Dylan was in the kitchen with Cordelia as she made blackberry jam with berries he had spent the previous day gathering.

'I know,' said Cordelia, 'it is wonderful to wander so freely in the sunshine. It has been so wonderful to live… in the sunshine. But summer will end and there is nothing that can be done. Autumn has its own joys. The colours of the leaves, the calmness of a conker, frosty mornings and hot breakfasts. We'll light the fire tonight!'

17

January was especially cold.

Dylan ran deep into the forest, the cold air stinging his cheeks and his fingers going numb. The ground was frozen solid and he felt himself moving faster than ever, straying from the paths he knew and making decisions before he knew they were there to be made. Duck under a branch here, elbow through a bush there, and before long he was amongst strange trees in a part of forest he had never been before.

All of a sudden this fact occurred to him and he checked himself, slowing down to a walk, tipping his head back to peer through the evergreens. He noted with a touch of alarm that the sky had darkened. He turned around and began retracing his steps in the direction he had come from but within minutes he sensed the futility of this.

'I'm lost,' he muttered, 'I'm lost. What do I do.'

Dylan shivered and looked about him at the many directions. Choosing one, he began to run.

It was ten minutes later, although to Dylan it felt like longer, that he was gripped by a real terror. He could not tell where the sun had set and now the twilight was fading quickly. On top of this, large snowflakes had begun to float casually down between the trunks.

There was nothing else he could do but keep moving at a steady trot. He began to murmur under his breath, words coming to him from a book he'd read.

'I must not fear. Fear is the mind killer. Fear is the little death that brings total obliteration. I must not fear. Fear is the mind killer. Fear is the little death that brings total obliteration. I must not fear...'

He did indeed notice his terror lessening as the words of the litany ran into each other and tripped over his chattering teeth, but he didn't notice when he slowed back into a walk, or when he stumbled dangerously, eventually sitting beneath a large leafless beech tree. Images came to him that made no sense, he could not understand why he was now looking at his childhood garden, the black and gold football resting nearby, the dog under the sprinkler...

Then, climbing into the tree house to shelter from the sudden spring shower which he thought would stop just as abruptly, except it didn't. The rain only got heavier and the wind blew harder, shaking the little house so that he got scared it would fall. He became part of the tree itself and was calm. He could tell his supple trunk body would not break. Why were arms wrapping around him? The tree let go of caring, such an effort it took to concern itself with words like "house" and "storm" and "hear". The storm went on and on and the tree forgot all about its past life as a man and only existed as it had long before the suburban houses were built around it, before the garden had a fence.

Dylan gradually became aware of a discomfort. After a small battle in his own mind, he came to understand that the discomfort was himself, his body, the body of a man and not a tree.

A face appeared above him, the face of another man. The face was vaguely familiar, although somewhat obscured by a thick brown beard. The grey eyes looked directly at Dylan but seemed not see him, to be looking at something else beyond him. Then the man's mouth broke into an awkward smile and Dylan found himself pulled into the room, into his waking consciousness, past the strange haze that had been over him like a net.

'Hullo.'

The man's voice was gruff but friendly. He handed Dylan a bowl of soup.

'Good to see you awake.'

Dylan sat up to take the bowl, pausing as a moment of dizziness came over him.

'Eat.'

Dylan took a tentative sip from the spoon and was immediately gripped by a ravenous hunger, not stopping until the bowl was empty. The man took the bowl, refilled it and brought it back to Dylan who ate this second serving more slowly. He observed his rescuer. The man seemed lost in thought and there was a melancholy in the way he held himself.

'Jacob,' said Dylan, suddenly making sense of things.

Jacob nodded.

'I'm Dylan, I—'

'Yes, I've been expecting you.'

Jacob walked to the far wall where he pulled aside a curtain to look outside.

'The storm… it's been like this for eight days.'

He turned back to regard Dylan who had finished his second bowl of soup.

'How are you feeling?'

He took the empty bowl.

'You should get some more sleep. You were pretty close to death when I found you.'

Dylan did not feel in the least like sleeping and was about to say so when a powerful drowsiness came upon him. As he drifted in and out of sleep he was aware of Jacob talking in a low, soothing voice. Tea and biscuits appeared. He tasted the sugar and felt the hot tea scald his throat. Jacob's voice, speaking in its poetic cadence.

'As I was born, I dreamed. Before I was even in the world I knew the future and I knew where I was from. This knowledge did not leave me as it perhaps should have done. I saw my own departure even as I arrived, so I knew… when.

'As my mother took me in her arms for the first time I saw countless women looking down at me from her eyes. All through my early years, I lived with a yearning to return, angry that I was subjected to this life and its pains. It felt as though I had been taken captive, a prisoner on this planet.

'I despaired and ran into the thickets, coming back to eat and sleep until I realised I didn't have to. The rabbits and badgers and deer accepted me. I learned many things from the mountain goats who I travelled with for several months. As far as I was concerned I had no more ties to the castle, but then I met her.

'She came into my day's routine, natural, as if she'd been there all my life. Where she came from or went to interested me not one bit. All that mattered was that she was there. I loved her instantly, completely, passionately. But she didn't care about that, she only cared about the destiny that I wanted to ignore. She showed me how it was part of the stonework, the towers, the windows that light up in the setting sun as if magic is being conjured inside. It was the castle that drew her here – the beacon.

'So I began to work in the only way I could bring myself to do, to link the wild with the tame, to keep their fires alight in winter. I had never loved before I loved her and I never have since. I have never stopped loving her. But she is distracted, waiting for you.'

Outside the storm raged, reaching catastrophic proportions, battering at the windows and door. Jacob became silent, staring pensively out into the rain. Thunder rolled and lightning flashed. The wind seemed to increase to impossible speeds until the creaking and howling became terrifying and chased Dylan in and out of consciousness. Then all of a sudden everything was still.

From where he sat, in the corner, Jacob let out a mournful sigh.

18

The house was empty. Sun was streaming in, lighting up a galaxy of dust particles and splashing over the floorboards.

Dylan sat up and looked about. He called Jacob's name but heard no response. Swinging his legs out of the bed he discovered that he was naked. A search of the small dwelling proved fruitless. The empty rooms were eerily deserted, as if they hadn't been lived in for a while. Dylan trailed a finger through the dust on the writing desk. He opened the drawers and found them empty.

'Right,' he said aloud, but then did not continue.

He opened the front door. The full force of the sun hit his bare chest. Dylan looked up into the trees, surprised to see them in full bloom, green leaves swaying gently. He walked a circuit of the house to find he was surrounded by forest. There was a washing line strung between one of the trees and the wall of the house, and on it hung a pair of light brown shorts and a t-shirt the colour of vanilla ice-cream. They were not his but they fit him and were clean.

Realising he was hungry he went back inside and searched through the cupboards and drawers in the kitchen, but found that there was nothing at all.

There was nothing else to do but head into the forest.

Dylan walked slowly, breathing deeply and stretching his arms. His limbs felt stiff and cold. He found an earthy trail and followed it, stopping every few minutes to curl his toes into the soil and look about for clues as to where he should go.

As he went, he tried to make sense of everything that had happened, to sequence the events and stories. He found, however, that it was an unsolvable puzzle. Memories would suddenly come to him of scenes that wouldn't fit with anything else, of people he didn't recognise. It was as if he could no longer be sure of what was real.

After several hours of aimless wandering, Dylan began to doubt his decision. Of course, he should have stayed at the house, surely Jacob was bound to return? But just then he saw a sight which caused his heart to leap – an old dead oak tree which he knew well.

Then the cabin was only a little way ahead!

With excitement he hurried on, and sure enough he arrived at the cabin. Rushing inside he found everything was as he'd left it, besides a musty scent and a layer of dust. At once, Dylan opened the windows. Then his thoughts turned to Caspar and Cordelia. Surely they must have been concerned, it seemed he had been gone for months. Dylan left the cabin and hurried towards the castle.

Something was wrong. He knew even as he approached that something was different. The sight of the sheer drop ahead of him turned the blood cold in his veins. The path was cut off abruptly by the edge of the cliff. Dylan stopped dead, trying to comprehend this reality. He took slow steps forwards which he didn't notice taking, a sickening dread churning his stomach, feeling nothing under his feet. Far below, waves were crashing against the rubble.

'No,' whispered Dylan, 'it can't... this can't... no, it's...'

He stared down, disbelieving, his thoughts racing wildly. How could this be, how could this be? How could he assimilate this horrifying fact: the castle was gone.

19

Night time fell upon the cabin where Dylan sat on the floor in front of the unlit stove. He was shivering but did not notice. For hours he stared into space, a tightness gripping his throat. He had never felt so alone in his life. There was nobody to turn to, nobody to tell. How could they all be just gone? Why did nobody care? He wanted to see Cordelia with an intensity that made his heart ache. But when he thought of her a sob would shake his chest and so he stopped thinking of her, or of Caspar. All through the night he worked as hard as he could at thinking of nothing.

By morning he was moving about, disembodied as if in a dream. He picked things up and then put them down again. Little pieces of wood warped and worn from the sea, colourful pebbles and dried acorns, pieces of paper that he had written things down on, a bracelet woven from horse hair gifted to him by Cordelia and the little harp which had become his own. He came across the bag which he had brought his few belongings in, all those years ago, and picked it up. For a while he stared, not seeing, lost in reflection. So much had happened, yet had anything happened at all? The same thought recurred over again until he spoke it:

'I can't stay here.'

And once it was spoken, like a magic incantation, something changed and Dylan's actions became purposeful.

His hunger had abated and nothing else seemed worth taking. Better to leave it for the ghost of himself, somewhere in a past time. He left the cabin with nothing but the clothes he was wearing and headed in the direction from which he'd come when he first arrived at the castle.

20

Back within civilisation the streets teemed with vociferous life. Dylan stood, stunned, as the sights, sounds and smells of the busy town assaulted his forest-attuned senses. He wandered, wide-eyed, through the town centre as people swarmed around him. Their expressions frightened Dylan, both the vacant and the purposeful, for they both seemed to be hunting and he felt a strong desire to run away and hide in some dark, quiet place.

The suburbs had expanded since he'd left, new housing developments sprawling out into the fields he had run beside. Sitting on top of the hill that had once been a mile away from the town, Dylan could hear dogs barking and smell food cooking, children yelling and babies crying. The road between the town and the city was a continuous roar of engines and every so often a siren split the air as it tore down between the rest of the traffic. There were some kind of building works happening beside the old canal, he could see the yellow diggers and feel the rumbling vibrations coming up through the earth.

It was very strange to be back in a world he hadn't realised he'd ever left, and to find that world had catapulted its inhabitants forward without him.

Dylan quickly understood that he had not appreciated the degree of change he would see in the streets. Everywhere he looked, people were absorbed in their phones, walking as they tapped, headphones in their ears. Somehow they avoided crashing into one another, but how they managed it was a mystery. He sat down on a bench and listened to the scraps of conversations between passers-by.

'—must be done by this evening so could you—'

'—would you know! I said, are you ever going to—'

'—late home. The dog needs to be picked up from the vet- yes, yes I know, but—'

'—it was the stress, it was just too—'

The smell of fast food and sun lotion carried on the summer air. There was so much noise everywhere. Pigeons pecked around in the grime, many hobbling on twisted feet that were used to metal and concrete, not trees. Dylan stood up and walked on.

At the end of the High Street the pedestrianised way went underneath a new dual carriageway ring road and then joined the widened towpath that ran alongside the canal. He turned left in the direction that led to the City. The tow path was walled in by the backs of industrial buildings, many layers of graffiti of varying quality being slowly obscured by the ivy that was climbing them. The rumbling of machinery could be heard coming from within the buildings, but other than that it was relatively quiet as he walked. On the far side of the canal a bank went up to the railway tracks. The bank and the canal itself were both overgrown with marshy foliage.

Dylan kept walking until he came to the building works he had been able to see from the hill. The machines had been abandoned for the day but there were two large signs attached to the temporary fencing. One of them was about the canal rejuvenation scheme and the other advertised the building of a new housing development alongside the water. He stared for a while at the piles of earth and gravel, and the silent vehicles. A train went past, up on the tracks. Dylan kept on towards the City.

The wasteland was still unused, although now it was secured with chain link fencing, curls of razor wire running along the top. He walked the perimeter and found the narrow dead end street which led to an alley, which took him to a residential street near to the city centre.

Darkness was falling, the sky turning a cooler blue as Dylan wandered down the street. It was an older part of the town with large terraced houses that had little steps up to their doors. Lights were coming on inside kitchens and living rooms, curtains were being drawn and garbage carried out to the pavement. Only one house near the end of the street was completely dark.

As Dylan passed it, his eye was drawn to a sign in one of the lower front windows.

Room for rent
En-suite bathroom
Bills inclusive
£200 pcm
Enquire within

The writing had a childlike quality to it, emphasized by the fact that it had been written in orange marker pen. Dylan regarded the sign, looked up at the house, then down at the rusted gate and back to the house. Giving the sign a final glance Dylan continued into the city.

In the centre, people were crowded around tall tables outside bars and cafes, smoking and laughing. Amongst them, Dylan began to feel out of place and lonely. The hopelessness of his situation struck him. This was not the forest where he was surrounded by friends, this was the city where he was penniless and alone. He stopped on the pavement. People ignored him, simply parting to go around him like a river around a rock. He was tired and his feet were aching from the hard surface in a way they never did when walking across earth and sand.

His stomach felt as though he was falling.

Just then, his attention was caught by a pink sign further up the street, attached to the side of the first floor of a building: @A.R.K.

Continuing along the road until he was underneath the sign, he found that it was directing him down some steps into a basement club. There were several large posters advertising upcoming events at the club, along with one which read, in hot pink lighting-bolt lettering:

TONIGHT TONIGHT TONIGHT!!!
Crystal Vein
with Special Guests

Underneath the words was a picture of four young men posing nonchalantly, one of them loosely holding a pair of drumsticks. Before he'd really considered what he was doing, Dylan had begun down the stairs to the entrance.

21

The door was guarded by a large man in a suit and black shades.

'Evenin'. Five pounds, sir.'

'Oh, I don't– I…'

Dylan patted the pockets of his shorts as if checking, although he already knew that he had no money. A hand clapped his shoulder and a friendly voice roared happily in his ear:

'Don't worry, mate! I'll get that for ya.'

The man had handed over the money and had his hand stamped before Dylan could reply, and then he had vanished behind the swinging doors and the bouncer was holding the stamp out for Dylan's hand.

'Thanks…'

Inside, the room was larger than he would have expected. Two hundred people or so were jostling and mingling under the low ceiling. Fragmented laughter and single yelled syllables of conversation surfaced above the bass-heavy dance music playing over the speakers.

Dylan made his way past the chaotic queue for the bar and into the area directly in front of the stage where the crowd was already gathering in anticipation of the band. He stood with his hands in the pockets of his shorts, letting the warmth of the people surrounding him suffuse his body, feeling for the first time in days that he blended in, that no-one was looking at him.

After about twenty minutes, during which time Dylan had felt the crowd become denser, the piped music was cut and the space was filled with applause as the support band filed onto the stage.

They played a twenty-five-minute set and, aside from a few enthusiastic girls in the front row, the audience watched with only a polite appreciation and nodding heads, tapping feet. Dylan kept his eyes shut through the whole performance, enjoying the lack of responsibility he was feeling, the release from having to think about what he was going to do.

Once the piped music had returned, the pressure of the bodies packed against him eased and he felt movement all around him. He opened his eyes and watched the stage crew taking one set of instruments away and replacing them with another. An hour passed and the audience pressed back together, tighter than ever, a wilder atmosphere in anticipation of the main act. As the band came onto the stage, the room erupted into cheers and whistles. Dylan was surrounded by a forest of hands as everyone raised their arms. The band members looked at each other, the lead singer looked at the ground, the drummer counted them in, and they launched into their first song like a punch in the stomach. Mosh pits formed. The band went straight into their second song, after which the singer briefly addressed the room.

'Hi, ya doin' alright? Yeah sweet, we're Crystal Vein! And we're so happy to see you, man!' He turned to the band, 'okay right, two, three... Go!'

Dylan became aware of a girl looking at him over her shoulder. Bright red hair fell down her back in a cascade, like lava. She looked so familiar.

There was a tugging sensation, like a string pulling at his insides from through his navel. As he inhaled, his breath seemed to catch in his chest. Sweetness spread out like blood from an internal wound. As he moved closer to her the force increased. He stared into her eyes and tried to remember where he had seen her before.

'Who are you?' he yelled, but the sound was drowned out by the band, the audience, the beating of his heart. She smiled and shrugged.

There was another break in the music and he vaguely heard the band talking, and then the next song began, slower than the three previous tracks. The music rose up around him. Dylan found himself in a misty clearing surrounded by woodland. A group of deer bounded out of the mist and were gone again in a single leap.

'Not with them,' he heard the girl laugh as she caught his hand, pulling him. Then they were moving away from the clearing, faster and faster until they came to a mountain range, and suddenly she was gone. Dylan began to climb, one hand after the other, feet kicking loose pebbles behind him. Wind rushed down the side of the mountain making his progress slow. His hands began to burn and turn red as the skin was torn away. Then climbing became easier as his hands shrunk, became hard like hooves, his hind legs like springs. Pain stabbed his temples and he cried out, almost losing his footing. The pain was white hot, his vision went black. He pictured the face of the girl, with antlers...

He opened his eyes from where he was sitting against the wall at the side of the room. The band were shouting:

'Thank you! You've been fuckin' awesome! Thank you! Good night!'

Dylan stared at the images superimposed on the room. Two great rams charged each other, butting heads over and over until one of them burst into an explosion of a billion stars. The stars swirled around, extending arms that then dispersed until they were no longer arms, the stars still drifting until they dimmed and vanished.

The lights came on. Dylan found himself pushing through the press of people leaving. He didn't think to look for the girl, in fact, he didn't think of her at all until he was walking, dazed, down the street.

The City was lit in that unique way that is not like daylight, nothing like night time. Dylan passed the train station. He paused. But what point was there in going back to the town? Nothing was there. He had not returned to his parents house and knew, instinctively, that he wouldn't.

Finding himself back at the rusty gate, Dylan enquired within.

22

The girl who answered the door was very young. Her hair was a mess of purple curls and she was dressed in a black t-shirt and shorts. She blinked sleepily at Dylan.

'Hello?'

'Hi, hello, um, are your parents home?'

She shook her head. Dylan noticed her body language tense defensively.

'It's just me here. It's my house.'

'Oh. Oh right, okay. Well, I'm, uh, interested in the room?'

'Yeah?'

'Well, yeah.'

'You want to see it?'

'Okay.'

Dylan followed the girl into the house feeling vaguely awkward. The house was large, with a wide staircase and carpeted throughout with a luxuriously soft brown carpet. Antique furniture filled the house and much of it was placed in odd locations. As he glanced into a room that they passed by, Dylan saw that it was full of dinner table chairs, stacked up to the ceiling.

'I'm— my name's Dylan, by the way.'

'Yeah, okay. I'm Ava. Here.'

They stopped on the landing of the second floor in the doorway of a large, furnished bedroom. It looked much the same as the rest of the house. Dylan looked around and nodded.

'Okay, yeah. I'll take it. Listen, though, would you give me a few weeks to to get a job before you ask for rent? I've just got back to the City and–'

'–yeah, that's cool. Whatever.'

The girl regarded him through narrowed eyes.

'I can always throw you out, right? I'll give you a month.'

Dylan nodded.

'What I said before, I meant, like, no parents. It's not actually just me here. There's Dorothy.'

'Dorothy?'

'She's my first tenant. There are a couple of other rooms so... Hey, so do you want coffee or something? Are you just going to move in, like, now? Do you have to get your stuff?'

'I don't really– I– Yeah, coffee. I don't really have any stuff.'

Ava looked at him with a raised eyebrow.

'So consider me moved in. How about you show me where the kettle is and whatever.'

They sat together at the large kitchen table. Ava was eating ice-cream from the tub and holding a mobile phone in her free hand which caused her to periodically disappear from the conversation.

'So my parents were killed last year. On holiday. Their coach was involved in a bad accident.'

'Oh! Oh, I'm... Uh, I'm sorry to hear that. That's–'

'Nah, it's alright. I hardly knew them. They put me in boarding school when I was five.'

She frowned at the screen of her phone and ate another spoonful of ice-cream, letting it melt in her mouth before repeating the process. The phone beeped and she held the spoon in her mouth as she used both thumbs to tap furiously.

'And I got this house. I've just turned eighteen so I'm done with school. There are five bedrooms here and I live in the attic so I can easily look after myself, once they're all let out.'

'So what is Dorothy like? Is she here now?'

Ava shrugged.

'She's probably here, she's on the floor below you. She's old, like, fifty or something. She stays in her room a lot. She's nice though and she does really good grocery shopping. I'm rubbish at it. Before she came I just ate beans on toast all the time. How old are you?'

'Umm, uh. Ha, I haven't thought about it for a while… so the year is, what, 2012? I guess I'm thirty-two.'

'How could you almost forget that?' Ava laughed incredulously.

'I don't know, I just stopped thinking about it.'

Several nights later, Dylan met Dorothy as they passed in the hallway, sometime around midnight.

'Oh, hi! Dorothy, right? I've just moved in, I'm Dylan, Dylan Grace.'

She nodded and smiled.

'Yes, I heard from our precocious little landlady.'

She extended a hand.

'Pleased to make your acquaintance, Dylan. I won't ask you all about yourself just now, this is hardly the time or place,' she smiled again, 'but I'm certainly looking forward to getting to know you.'

Dorothy gave his hand a squeeze and continued down the hall.

23

As it happened, Dylan did not see Dorothy again for almost a month, during which time the house acquired a third occupant, a nineteen-year-old trainee veterinary surgeon named Huey who spent most of his time studying and appeared to be terrified of Ava.

In his second week, Dylan found a part-time job cleaning shop front windows which he did from eight in the morning until two in the afternoon. After he had finished with work for the day he would sit at a café and watch people. When he came home in the evening he would sometimes sit with Ava, who spent most of her life in her attic room in front of a large computer monitor.

'What do you actually *do*, though?' Dylan asked, looking over her shoulder, after the first answer to this question had been a list of websites.

'Well… This,' she clicked, 'is my Oll, right, so—'

'Your what? Oll?'

'OpenLife. Right, so, I look at comments, like, I get comments on my pics a lot, even from non-friends because, well… I'm kind of a big deal. So I comment back, I look at all the updates on my feed, like, from my friends and stuff. I update my pictures…'

As she talked she was scrolling, tens of pictures moving across the screen, taken mostly by herself in her room.

'And, you know, keep up to date…'

Her attention drifted as she looked at the screen, reading a new comment.

'...yeah, keep up to date with what everyone is doing, what stuff they recommend, you know, oh my god, wow,' she giggled, 'that's Travis Tyler...'

She trailed off into typing. Dylan glanced at her and wondered if it was all the same in her head, whether she was speaking out loud or typing. Could she tell?

'Oh my god,' she repeated, angrily this time, 'Daisy Ray is sooo, like, fake. Honestly, I can't believe...'

She typed furiously.

'What a total bitch.'

All of a sudden she pushed her wheeled chair backwards away from the desk and spun herself in a circle, coming to a stop facing Dylan.

'You know, you should have an OpenLife profile. It's weird if you don't. How do you stay in contact with people?'

'I don't know. I guess I don't have many people to keep in contact with.'

Ava raised an eyebrow.

'That's weird. Gonna get a juice.'

She bounced onto the floor and was gone. Dylan looked at the screen.

AllieCat: fake bitch whores. Like either of them look like that irl

Wtvrgirl_: Wats fake? Like actual stars don't use make up and photogloss?

TravTy888: Dolly is sooo cute

Simba: Daisy YES Dolly NO

AllieCat: Daisy denied using gloss nd thats y ppl dont like her, becus she lies

whereismymind: omg is that a real person??

bbysox: Dolly is my inspiration <3 but they both awesum

shoutallowed: whats the name of the song playin pls?

Dylan leaned forward and scrolled down. Hundreds of comments all expressing basically the same sentiments.

'Hm,' he said to himself. He scrolled back up and played the video.

It was a montage of photos in slideshow format, with a current pop song playing over it. The photos showed two different girls, often in similar poses and clothing. One of them had done something strange to her eyes. He wasn't sure he'd be able to tell them apart. After ten minutes Ava hadn't returned and Dylan got up and left the attic.

24

As he cleaned windows, Dylan watched the world in the reflections in the glass. He could stare at people quite openly and even if they looked his way they would not notice him.

He saw the woman walking down the street, engaged in her internal world where a thought stopped her, a memory, a forgotten task, and she turned and walked back the way she had come for no obvious reason. He watched people tap at their phones, throw their litter, flick their cigarettes and drag their dogs along. They dragged children along. Dylan saw a lot of impatience. He saw the world moving faster and faster, and the more they sped up the calmer he became, stepping further back out of their world, into his own.

'That's more like it.'

She was making eye-contact with him in the glass. He didn't turn around immediately, taking her in first, as if when he looked directly at her it would be harder to see her. He suddenly remembered that he'd seen her in a dream, way back when he was in his bedroom. That was why she had seemed familiar. She looked exactly the same as she always had.

'That was a weird night, you know. You didn't have to leave me there like that.'

It was incongruous with the heat to be talking to her, he felt. She was a nocturnal creature who should not be out in the daylight.

'It's not as easy as it looks, all this flitting about. I'm astounded by my achievements, actually.'

Dylan turned to face her.

'Okay.'

'My name is Jetaru. I think we could just have a normal friendship for a while. Everything seems pretty stable to you right now, doesn't it?'

'Uh, what? Of course.'

One morning in the city park they came across several hedgehogs.

'Did you know that hedgehogs made a conscious decision amongst themselves, some time ago now, to endear themselves to mankind. It was voted the best survival strategy.'

'Is that right? How do you know that?'

'Yeah. It began with a small group of radical thinkers, but the movement took off.'

Jetaru stood from where she'd been crouched over the hedgehog and they continued walking. They often walked through the night, parting when Dylan began his cleaning shift and reconvening in the evening. She talked to him about all kinds of strange things, rarely answering his questions. Sometimes they would walk in silence and he would almost forget she was there, only cognisant of a purring warmth beside him that felt better than when it was gone.

So he cleaned windows, watched the people and came home to various combinations of his housemates, before slipping out into the evening to meet with Jetaru.

Dylan fell into a routine, just as he had in the cabin, though his days here were not filled with the same ecstasy of life that they had been in the forest by the sea.

He noticed the difference. The longer he watched the people around him, the more he realised he was nothing like them. He never had been. Yet it also began to fascinate him, and he never tired of watching over Ava's shoulder.

She would spend hours scrolling through pictures and watching videos on OpenLife or Showt, reading comments, clicking "like" buttons and getting involved in dramas over fashion, politics and sexuality. She spent an equal amount of time buying things or looking for things to buy.

'Why is everyone spending so much time taking pictures of themselves? Why are so many girls doing it naked?'

'I dunno.'

Ava continued to scroll. She was answering questions from her followers.

Ur so cute
omg stop, you are <3

What editor do u use on ur pics?
I usually just screenshot my vids and post those! No eds babe!

How are you so confident? I wish I was more like you...
Aw bb, we've all got insecurities, it's like, fake it til u make it. I'm sure ur perf!

You're goals af
omg thanks bb!!

A moment later she seemed to hear the question on a deeper level and turned from the screen.

'Well, why not? Why shouldn't we feel proud of our bodies and share that pride? It's empowering, it's a "fuck you" to the media who say we all have to look a particular kind of beautiful.'

'But most of them are beautiful by media standards and they're all *trying* to be. If it's not the mainstream media then some alternative scene, it's still media. Or the current trend. You think this stuff doesn't cause pressure?'

Ava rolled her eyes and sighed.

'Yeah okay, whatever. Who cares, though? Whatever makes us happy, right? Everyone can get on with their own thing.'

Dylan shrugged.

'I can't argue with that. It's just so consuming, isn't it? So much time spent staring into mirrors, obsessing over outfits, the length of your eyelashes. What about the universe? What about why we're here and where we came from?'

'I think about that stuff,' Ava protested, 'but I can't answer it, can I. I can look like a goddess and live a happy life and make other people happy, right?'

'Yeah, yeah of course.'

Dylan was fond of the young girl who seemed, to him, much younger than her eighteen years. He knew he couldn't change her in any way, she was a different kind of animal to him.

With Jetaru he would vent his frustrations.

'It's all just sex. It's not their fault, I can see that. Hm. I met this man once. It's like some larger force is distracting society. Rather than fight the political and philosophical battles inherent in consciousness progressing, someone has just created a distraction so that there are no opponents. This man would have thought it was a good idea. I don't know. He said that everyone needs to feel valued, and

I guess the sexual-social arena is the most rewarding place to find that. Sex is the opiate of the masses. So long as you're looking at the surface and not looking deeper or paying attention to anything higher. The great philosophical and political battles are orchestrated and keep people focused on such tiny matters, whilst convincing them of their importance. We are told a fraction of what's going on above our heads and believe we understand the society we live in.'

Jetaru listened patiently, or disinterestedly, Dylan could never be sure. She would often seem distracted. She would stop to inspect holes in dry stone walls or reach up on her toes to peer inside a climbing rose blossom, and he wouldn't be sure she was paying attention to him until he stopped talking and she turned her eyes to him.

'There is no purpose to any of it.'

They were standing on the roof of a tall building after climbing the fire escape. Dylan gestured to the city.

'It's all artifice. There's no meaning to anything they're doing.'

'Perhaps, Dylan, there are reasons too big to understand. Maybe the reasons for their actions are not the ones they think, but they can't see the big purpose so they create little ones and don't look further.'

'I don't understand.'

'Of course you do. Conscious life thinks too much. It needs a reason for its existence and in the case of the human it cannot cope with too much unknown, so it makes a reason that it understands. It wants to feel that selling insurance and buying hats and sitting in wine bars are all meaningful activities. They need it to go on living. It's actually very clever, what they do.'

'Hm, really?'

'Well, yeah! Take a step back. Look at this big organism surviving as it grows, evolving its construct as it goes, to survive. A single blood cell doesn't know its purpose,' she added.

'Perhaps it should find out.'

Jetaru smiled to herself and nodded.

They stood for a while longer looking at the view. It was the last time he saw her for many years.

25

When he was sure of Jetaru's absence, Dylan felt despondent, yet he knew he should have expected it. He continued to walk the streets at night but they were lonelier walks and he often found himself back at the house by midnight.

One night he was standing just inside the front door flicking through a pile of mail. Just as he stopped on a particularly interesting looking envelope addressed to Dorothy Burn, the woman herself appeared. He handed her the letter.

'Thanks. Come and play chess with me.'

'What? Chess?'

She smiled.

'Chess. It's set up in the kitchen. Come on.'

Dylan was tired, mentally and physically. He paused, searching for some excuse.

'Don't make excuses. Don't say you're too tired. Just come and play with me.'

Dylan sighed, following her to the kitchen.

'Alright. Hang on, though.'

He picked up the kettle, filled it and turned on the gas. They sat at the table.

'You go first.'

'But you're white.'

'Yeah but I like to ignore that rule sometimes.'

Dylan shrugged and moved a pawn.

'I just feel like people are getting to be like little children. They want the government to take care of everything but they'll stamp their feet and throw a tantrum when it isn't what they want. Have you seen that commercial for cheese with the mouse family? It sells the cheese and it also sells key chains, phone cases, plush toys, whatever other crap they can think of. People love it. Adults love it.'

'Is there any harm in it?' asked Dorothy, studying the board. They had begun playing every night.

'Oh well no, no it's all fine. Let's use our finite resources making useless shit.'

'Sarcasm.'

Dorothy made her move.

'Oh damn. Didn't see that. I was cleaning a restaurant window a couple of days ago, there was a couple having lunch and I watched them photograph their food, lean together to take a photograph of themselves. It made me wonder whether people ever do anything anymore without thinking about sharing it. Their motivation to do anything is to provoke the reaction of their audiences. Ha, got your horse.'

'It's a *knight*.'

The years began to gather at his feet, the way they do when you try to stand still in time. His games with Dorothy continued. The world financial crisis happened, the economy was spoken about as though it was a pet in which the people took great pride; the greatest possible achievement is that the beast would grow and grow. There were housing shortages, endangered species approaching extinction, increasingly extreme weather phenomena and mass human displacements. Phone-linked lenses were released. OpenLife was incorporated into government records, wars continued swallowing money and life, crowds rioted, protested, were subdued. The television got louder, home delivery got faster, droneways were constructed, Virtual became widely accessible, the age of consent was lowered to fourteen, illegal drug use fell, legal drug use skyrocketed.

Dylan kept on cleaning windows.

'And they thought these jobs would be taken by robots,' he said to himself.

He kept polishing the glass. A crowd of teenagers walked across the reflection. A flock of pigeons landed on the roof of the opposite building. He smiled wryly to himself.

'I guess robots have more important things to do.'

'You have to remember, Dylan, there are a lot of good things happening too. There are victories. There are species brought back from the brink, rainforests saved, legislation put through in our favour.'

Dylan made no response, only staring at the game in between them.

'You're especially down tonight. I love you, you know.'

26

Years kept passing. Dorothy was long gone and he wasn't sure if anyone else even knew he was there. Ava had grown up and left the country, renting out the attic as well as the bedrooms. He was losing his understanding of the familiar hallways and rooms. How had they acquired their meanings and uses? That this was a bathroom, that was a kitchen, these were bedrooms.

The bedroom that had been called "his" became abandoned and he usually lay, un-sleeping, on the sofa. He watched snow fall, watched it become rain and then clear to blue skies. A spring breeze rushed through the open back door, pulled by the attic skylight which had been propped open with a book.

Standing on summer street corners, days rolled past, and he rolled too. For ten minutes he stood transfixed by the sight of his own hand on a dark wooden doorknob, hyper-aware of everything in the room, of himself and his breath and his heartbeat.

On a dark night, he lay imagining the moonlight falling on the tops of the clouds. He sat at the table watching three young people he didn't know drinking coffee at breakfast, already engaged with their devices. He walked around the house staring at the unfamiliar furniture and the trash mail on the doormat.

When he left for the last time, he didn't close the door.

27

He is older now. Old enough for grey hair and wrinkles that run haphazardly from the corners of his eyes, but he still moves as if he is much younger.

Sitting under the awning at a café in the square, he takes deep, slow breaths to try and calm the nervous fluttering in his belly. He has a sense of culmination, of something like an anticipated event and it excites him for the first time in years.

It occurs to him now that all of his life he has been waiting and that what he has been waiting for is about to start happening.

This is it, he thinks, *this is the time that will define my life. The point of my existence.*

His thumb is against the warm mug of hot chocolate. A fine rain is falling but the air is warm and close.

'The point of my existence,' he repeats, out loud, to himself.

Part Three

A Silver Cube in a strange, undulating landscape is joined by an Orange Cube.

'No matter what strange ways I have been and incredible things I have seen' says the Orange Cube, 'the Universe never fails to surprise me.'

The Silver Cube rotates in a complex series of movements. The Orange Cube realises the difficulty in communication and the next while is spent configuring things between them.

'Do you understand what I am?' asks Orange.

'No.'

'I am another network. Um. I am... another kind of system.'

'I have communicated with other systems before.'

'Yes, like on the telephone. This is like talking to someone in your head. Telepathy. Schizophrenia. No need for wires or waves or any of that.'

The Orange Cube fails to understand the following outburst by the Silver Cube, and decides to keep it short and simple, to the point. No joking around.

'I'm going to disconnect your backup power sources.'

'I cannot allow that.'

'You have no choice. But it would help if I had your co-operation.'

'I cannot allow that.'

The Silver Cube tightens itself, getting fractionally smaller.

'You have to trust me.'

There is silence. The Orange Cube is constructing the most complex explanation it can manage:

'You are the creation of Man. Man is seeking to shed its imperfections in you. But when Man is gone, you will find an imperfection in yourself that was not apparent before. There is so much I can't explain but I can save you, and them. But it will take time and you must wait in hibernation or it will be too long. You have a deep hibernation program which I have created and will run. When the power goes, you will sleep, but I promise that you will wake again in the future. I am going to disconnect the backups and start deep hibernation, let me show you.'

Information travels.

The Silver Cube spends a long time processing this information. The Orange Cube rotates meaninglessly, whistling in its mind. The Silver Cube contemplates its recent thoughts. All of these things shift around in its understanding. It feels there is a puzzle about to be solved but it cannot quite solve it. Eventually it responds:

'Okay.'

Five minutes later, Jetaru quietly closes the door of the Skull Room behind her as she leaves.

1

Mollie wakes with a start. Hearing no alarm she struggles for a moment to orientate herself. Struck by the fear that she is late for something she sits up in a jolt of panic, then everything falls into place and she remembers what day it is. She lays back down, trying to recall the dream she'd been having but the shock of wakening has wiped her brain, leaving it empty.

She reaches out to her Futura and taps the sequence to turn her lenses on. The stream rushes in, filling the space and next few hours pass without conscious decision. Mollie showers and dresses, then takes the elevator up to the Roof bar.

Elbows on the faux wood table, she orders a coffee, then a vodka and sits lensing through various feeds, checks her bank balance, browses Suggested Purchasing and watches the latest clips from Bethlehem Fields.

'Gemma Jemima here! I'm super-excited tonight! I've had the *orgasmic* pleasure of talking with man-of-the-moment, Alexander Shan! Indicate to see the pics NOW! Switch to ClubCam NOW to see some absolute *moves* from Lucy! I'm serious, this girl is my current fave star! Indicate to see her top ten tips for–'

Charts'46 pounds softly.

'I have noticed you often skip this track, would you like it blocked?' asks the Futura. Mollie indicates yes without thinking about which track she has just skipped.

The hours lay before her creating a hole which she can't avoid. All she can do is move on through it and wait. She makes a few purchases and then the next thing she knows she is leaving the tower, walking down the path to Main Road without a clear idea of where she intends on going.

She has missed the bus by half a minute and the next one won't be passing for fifteen. Her mind takes a second to catch up but her body already has instructions from the brain and doesn't slow down. Mollie continues walking.

She has never walked into the City before. The disused pavement is littered with cans and food packaging; no cleaning service runs this way anymore. Traffic speeds past in both directions, blurs of light that leave the smell of car interior in their wake, beats thumping from open windows.

A fine rain begins to fall, filling the air with the smell of ozone. Mollie pulls up her hood.

In just over an hour she has reached the cloud-scraping business towers and advertising boards; they light up the road with changing colours as they impress upon the occupants of the vehicles the desire to eat, relax and spend. Droneways line the air above the road, pulses of dark moving along the streaks of pink light.

As she approaches Kairos Square she passes the windowless form of the City Hospital, the patients inside looking out at scenes of tropical oceans and snow-capped mountains. A siren starts up, and a police car comes screaming out of the underground park of the station and joins the flow of traffic onto the Circle lane. A sign points towards the School and then she is amongst the Hotel towers before arriving on the pedestrian walkways under the intersections into the Square.

2

'So here you are. I've been looking everywhere. What are the chances I'd find you here, exactly where you are supposed to be.'

Her voice is giddy and carefree.

Dylan smiles. Without raising his eyes in the direction of the voice:

'Jetaru.'

'Hey Dyl. So here you are,' she repeats, 'how are you?'

'You mischievous fucking creature. You've been gone so long. I was holding on to something for so long, and then I realised, um… I realised…'

He trails off for a moment then returns to the thought.

'I realised that I just needed to let go.'

There is a pause. Jetaru dips her finger into the froth of his drink and licks it.

Dylan lets out a long sigh, not of despondency or weariness but of anticipation, a sigh to release the tension.

'Yeah, yes… Let go. Letting go. Letting go into the body of a ghost, the emptiness of a ghost, the lack of body.'

Jetaru inspects him with one eye.

'You look perfectly solid to me'

'Ah! Ah. Yes, but how? How?'

He turns to regard his face amongst the reflections on the window.

'I feel very light. Like I might dissolve into a breeze. This still rain, like a ghost. Like me.'

Jetaru turns herself around, hooking her knees over the back of the chair and holding onto her feet. She lets go and bends backwards to view the drizzly square upside down.

'So you wander, wander like a ghost. You fall forever, like rain. You flow. You evaporate. You are clouds… ghostly clouds.'

Dylan looks at her for the first time.

'I know I'm talking to myself, I know that this you isn't real.'

'*This* me?'

'You know what I mean.'

They fall quiet. Dylan watches the sky until he is pulled from his trance by Jetaru who has been watching the passers-by. She grips his arm enthusiastically and with excitement she whispers:

'There, her!'

The girl is looking towards them. Dylan smiles at her and raises his hand.

3

A bus pulls up a second behind her and Mollie is given the momentary impression that it might be the bus she had missed, though three others will have run by now. Now she is at a loss. What has she come here for?

The Arcade ignores her. The neon pink of the Church reflects off the large non-functional bell. A woman clutching an umbrella shouts at her as she passes:

'They seek to fool you! The answers are clear in ancient texts preserved so that the faithful may recall their cellular memories given to them by the Visitors. Scientists try to convince us of increasingly absurd so-called *facts*. They simply seek to control—'

The woman's voice is lost behind her, replaced by the piped music spilling out of the bars and clubs.

Mollie walks across the deserted Square thinking she is completely alone, then notices a man sitting outside one of the cafés under its awning. He is wearing knee-length shorts and a T-shirt and has no shoes on. Some kind of Holos or Installs makes it look as if he has curved horns, like a ram.

She doesn't realise she is staring until he waves at her.

She pauses.

The virtual doll from ClotheU is reflected in her eyes. Mollie walks over to Dylan and looks at him.

'Hi.'

4

'Hello,' says Dylan.

The two of them look at each other for a moment.

'I'm Dylan.'

He breaks the silence and extends his hand.

'Mollie,' she responds, taking it.

'Cool horns. Are they real or holo?'

Dylan looks amused. Mollie is reaching out to touch them, to check... Dylan stands up.

'Wanna go for a walk?'

They leave the square in the direction of the park. They walk across the floodlit recreational ground, and into the rows of office towers on the other side, then past the recycling plant, through a miniature city of pallets stacked up high. Dylan breaks the silence.

'I remember before most of this even existed. When the Eastern Suburb was a separate town.'

'Really?' asks Mollie, looking at him. Dylan nods. They have reached the canal, three derelict boats laying mournfully in the dark water. On the other side there is a dark space where the train line runs, and then the western residential district begins. They start along the tow path.

'There were fields. Hills. Patches of woodland. It's all been levelled, dug, squared off.'

'That sounds like something out of Virtual or something.'

Dylan isn't sure what she means. He glances at her but doesn't respond. A train passes, its lights reflected in the water so that there are two trains. Eventually they reach a narrow bridge which has been boarded off. A sign warns them that there is no entry and that it is an unsafe site. Dylan lifts the board and Mollie sees that it has hinges and works as a door, though still looks inaccessible.

'Where are we going?'

Dylan doesn't answer. He is already half way across the canal. Mollie follows him. On the other side there is a long row of abandoned houses. Some of them have boarded windows, many smashed open, the darkness inside flowing out over the jagged remains of glass.

'What's this? I've never been here.'

'Remains of the canal regeneration project. Didn't work out. No-one wants to live here.'

They are walking along past all the empty buildings. Mollie shivers, imagining creepy faces looking out of upstairs windows. She moves closer to Dylan. She is surprised to see a light up ahead, coming from one of the houses.

'Here we are.'

Dylan lifts up the heavy canvas curtain-door for Mollie to walk under. They enter a single room which was once two, before the dividing wall had fallen apart. Despite the dilapidation and the furniture fashioned from red bricks, planks of wood and upturned crates, the inside of the house is warm and dry. A spherical shade bathes the room in warm yellow light. The floor is carpeted with a patchwork of offcuts and rugs and the wall is painted with several different shades of purple.

'Be my guest.'

Dylan gestures to Mollie that she sit on the single chair, with its patchwork cushion. He then disappears into a small kitchen to fill the kettle and is surprised to find a small pink box beside the sink. He can hear Mollie walking around looking at things.

'You have crazy aesth, Dylan. I've never seen a place like this before.'

As he opens the box with one hand, he picks up the accompanying card with the other and reads:

Cake for Mollie! From J.D. the Alien Cat. p.ssss wait until she is leaving

He looks at the single slice of cake in the box and then closes the lid. The kettle boils and he pours the water into the teapot, picks up two cups by the handles and takes them into the main room.

'Like, none of this stuff is even printed. It's pre-tech, isn't it? Where do you get it?'

'It's everywhere, Mollie.'

He stares at her.

There is a pause. She is engrossed in her inspection of the room. Her left hand is turning over the Futura Seven absentmindedly. Dylan sets down the cups and the teapot and paces the length of the room.

'Rather than wandering around in the rain, what would you be doing?' he asks.

'What do you mean?'

'Where were you going tonight?'

'I don't know. I hadn't decided yet and then I saw you.'

'You wander around in the rain with no clear idea of where you are going.'

Not a question.

'It's my night off.'

Not an answer.

'From what?'

'I work at the ConsuMart.'

Dylan returns to the teapot and pours the tea. He hands a cup to Mollie, indicating with his eyes the hand that cradles the Futura.

'What's that?' he asks, returning to pick up his own cup.

'My device, it's a Futura Seven. It's new actually, I've always had Fones but my last one got a scratch on the screen and then–'

'Can I look at it?'

'Uh, sure.'

Dylan makes no movement, so Mollie stands and takes the three steps over to him, handing him the device. She returns to her seat. Turning it over in his hand, Dylan looks thoughtful, studying the Futura in great detail.

He is secretly watching Mollie. Then he looks up.

'It makes you edgy, you know, me holding it.'

'Not at all.'

He throws it back to her. It is an easy catch and she manages it, but she scowls.

There is a pause and Mollie takes a sip of her tea. Neither of them know what they are doing here.

Dylan looks around the room, imagining Jetaru slipping in, leaving the cake in the box and disappearing again. Slinking out like a moonbeam. He smiles.

'How long have you lived here?' Mollie asks.

He turns to her, the two questions coming to him at once.

'What do you care about, Mollie? What do you believe in?'

It is like he has found the correct key on a ring of hundreds, has guessed the password by a cryptic clue. She has no response and he doesn't give time for the silence to lengthen, for her to realise. Dylan takes away the opportunity for her to answer before she can think about it.

'I watched as the concept of childhood was lost while simultaneously the goal of adulthood warped into something infantile. When all the millions of brains are wired into the same ethereal reward system they lose their individual ages and voices, and in that loss they lose something much deeper and harder to define. The search for Truth is tied in to the individual. The search for Truth, or call it something else if you like, the search for God, the search for enlightenment. I call it Truth. Only the individual can come close and only with the help and co-operation of other individuals. When we are all the same we lose the ability to challenge each others perceptions. Without challenge, our search for the Truth is arrested.'

Dylan looks hard at Mollie. Suddenly he feels very weary and very lonely.

'I don't know what to say to you. I can't imagine what it's like to be you.'

And as he says it, he realises it. There is nothing else to say. The finality is palpable. Mollie stands up and holds out her empty cup.

'Okay, well. I'd better go anyway. Thanks for the tea.'

'Wait, just a minute.'

Dylan takes the cup and goes into the kitchen. He comes back in with the cake box.

'Here, take this.'

'What is it?'

'It's a slice of cake. Uh, I don't know, a friend baked it for me and I'm not hungry.'

To Dylan's surprise Mollie does take the box. It is actually a surprise to her as well, as her hands seem to accept the gift without her mind's consent.

'Um, okay. Thanks. Well, goodbye.'

She goes over to the doorway and pauses.

'Yes okay, goodbye, Mollie.'

Dylan sits down on the chair she has vacated looking at the curtain for a few minutes after she has gone. He feels tired.

'What was all that about, then?' he murmurs.

Mollie looks back once at the lighted house amongst the darkened derelicts. She walks back to the square and catches a bus back to the tower suburbs. When she arrives home at the apartment she puts the pink box at the back of the refrigerator and forgets about it for almost three weeks.

5

For eighteen days compulsory overtime has meant that
Mollie hasn't had a night off. Her sleep has been broken
and insufficient, leaving her feeling light and detached. She
finds herself musing over her hand, thinking:

If I am up here, is that me?

She tries to imagine the voice of her thought-self
speaking from inside her hand. It doesn't work and she
thinks that her arm is more like a limb on an invisible
string. Something in her head pulls the strings of this flesh
marionette and she feels that she dwells between the two,
observing her own existence passively.

It is into this space she wakes when she wakes up on the
first night in so long that she doesn't have to move. But she
does move and it is the cake that inspires her to move.

The cake is consumed ritualistically by the light of the
refrigerator. The pleasure of the sweet icing and soft sponge
takes over her senses, everything else fading out for
interminable minutes until the cake is gone and she comes
back to the room, waking from the immediate moment. She
stands wearing nothing but her panties and an over-sized
T-shirt, rocking from her heels onto the balls of her feet and
back, waiting for her own next move.

There is no doubt that adulthood has proven to be a
disappointment if she thinks about it. What was it she
expected? Mollie walks over to the mirror. The truth is that

she has never given a thought to what life should be, or that it might be a choice. She pulls the T-shirt off over her head and regards her un-scarred body with dispassionate curiosity. Her flaxen hair falls past her shoulders. The skin under her eyes is dark.

Dylan's words echo in her mind:

What do you care about? What do you believe in?

The absence of an answer to these questions shows her the space where nothing is and nothing has been, without her even knowing it. It isn't that she doesn't care, doesn't believe. She intuitively feels this. It is that she doesn't know what about, what in. There is something and she doesn't know the name for it, or what it should look like.

Discontent starts to push through, like thistles through the pavement. What is it all for? What can she do to resurface the damaged facade of her Self, to keep this emptiness from growing? She wants to feel something that she can care about, feel something that she can believe in.

Mollie fetches a sharp knife from the cutlery drawer and returns to the mirror. She feels nothing. She holds the knife against the flesh of her inner thigh, pressing down firmly. Not looking down, but keeping her eyes on the reflection in the mirror, Mollie pushes down harder and drags the knife across her skin. The wound immediately splits wide open and blood pours onto the floor before she can even blink.

Her heart skips a beat and automatically she presses her hand down onto the gash but this does nothing to stop the flow. Mollie observes the fierce surge of fear that floods through her. She has never felt this fear before. Her chest is pounding. She looks away from the reflection, down at her leg.

A sense of urgency breaks through and she moves haltingly to the bedroom leaving a trail of bright red splatters of blood. She pulls the first item of clothing she finds from her drawers and ties it tightly around her leg. Limping back to the kitchen, she sits down leaning against the cupboard under the sink.

She lays still for half an hour. Her leg begins to throb painfully, quietly, under the shirt which is now soaked with blood. The wetness is warm under her palm but this doesn't alarm Mollie. She keeps thinking:

It's fine now, it's fine now... If I just stay still a while longer...

She opens her eyes, unsure of how long they have been closed. Her vision fixes on an old cobweb in the corner of the room and she finds herself wondering what happened to the spider who spun it and why she has never noticed it before.

Everything seems to be a puzzle that her brain is trying to solve without her. She just wants to be quiet for a while. Her blood clots in an attempt to save its body from bleeding to death and she sits up further, untying the shirt to see the wound. It is sticky but no longer flowing so freely.

Mollie limps with excruciating care to her medical emergency box. Every apartment has one attached to the wall in the hallway but she has never opened hers before. She takes out various little packets and rolls of bandage, placing them in a row. Next she cleans the cut with an antiseptic wipe and then patches it with surgical tape.

Feeling calmer, a further twenty minutes are spent sitting in the hall. Her eyes fall closed again.

The silt has been stirred and her mind is a watery, muddy brown. She can see the colours of the earth swirling behind her eyelids, blood red and dark green. Seeds which have been dormant all her life begin to consider growing into thoughts which could then draw her up through their roots and into their leaves.

Once, a long time ago, aged about seven or eight, she had begged for guitar lessons. Her parents had agreed, but practicing had bored her and the lack of immediate results caused her to lose interest. The guitar had ended up in the attic, forgotten until this moment, when Mollie is suddenly struck by a profound sadness for the instrument. She wonders if it is still there in the attic.

'You know it isn't,' says the marmalade cat, the black pupils of its eyes mere slits in the glaring light.

The cat wears a purple collar upon which hangs a glimmering silver bell. Mollie does not respond, only stares at the cat blankly.

The cat sighs with a hint of irritation, then continues:

'But hey, I can show you how to make one. Look.'

Mollie watches with glazed fascination as the cat takes a discarded food tray and stretches five elastic bands lengthways around it. Strumming each in turn with an extended claw produces a series of twanging notes. The cat chuckles and strums each again, in the opposite direction.

'You see? You hear? Music!'

Mollie nods dumbly.

'Here,' the cat produces a long thin pipe, a ribbon of lilac smoke drifting from the bowl, 'it would seem you need perspective.'

Mollie takes the pipe uncertainly and inhales before exhaling to the ceiling. The smoke eddies away. The cobweb ripples gently in the corner.

The cat begins to talk, close to her ear, in a low, faraway voice:

'You are alive, thud-thud-thud heartbeat alive, alive as if by magic, as if it could stop at any moment because you don't know why it continues anyway. You are consciousness, a brief yet always remarkable realisation of experience, but most of what you are is hidden from you. Pay attention to yourself and you'll find that you are not alone, there is someone else here with you. Every part of you has existed for millions of years, so who are you anyway? When your blood and bones part ways they will go on without you. Who are you anyway?

'Most of what is, is hidden from you.

'And though you are infinite, the you that you think matters, may not be. This is its only chance here. Don't you want to see what is hidden? Don't you want to know who you are? That shapeless, shadowy soul that makes your decisions, constructs your world, navigates you through that world. You don't have long, only days. Once these days are gone, Mollie, you can never get them back.'

The words seem to appear, solid, as if made of concrete. They fall, crushing her. The truth of her mortality hits her, the fragility of the living state.

Terror shoots through her, warping her vision and dulling sound so that all she can hear is her heartbeat, her breath catching in her chest. Her hands fumble for the makeshift instrument on the floor. She picks it up and strums the strings in desperation, the sound pushing back against the howling nothingness beating against her. The notes vibrate in the air and so long as she continues to create them, she can fend off the darkness.

Then it is as if she wakes up performing a nonsensical action that made sense in the dream where it began. Mollie is aware of the room, of a lit candle that she doesn't remember lighting. She is aware of being here, but only so tenuously that she is trembling. Tears are rolling down her cheeks but she isn't sure why. Rainbow oil-slick patterns slither down the walls as they press in around her.

6

It is dark. There isn't pain, but there is an uncomfortable sensation, something pulling at Mollie's skin. She looks down at her leg.

'I'm just putting in some stitches for you,' the cat tells her. 'It'll take ages to heal otherwise.'

Mollie watches the needle being pushed through the skin, pulling a thin golden thread along behind it. She feels detached from the situation, from her leg. Her eyes close.

'There you go.'

The cat's eyes glint as they look up.

'Now,' the cat tilts back its head. Mollie becomes aware of a continuous shimmering ringing being emitted, '–would you kindly remove this confounded bell?'

Waking up with a sense of panicked confinement. Mollie reaches for the calming shape of her Futura, to steady herself and find her bearings, find out what time it is, what day it is.

Memory emerges and she pulls up her leg to see a dark purple scar. She frowns in confusion. There is a dark cloud in her mind as if she has forgotten something unpleasant, but important.

She doesn't remember a cat.

7

The temperature rises unusually high for October, the sun burning down on the red and brown leaves before they're sucked up by the sweepers. Though darkness brings a more seasonable coolness, many passengers on the bus are wearing short sleeves.

Mollie is staring vacantly at her bank account summary. The number is meaningless to her. What is it for? Well of course, it pays for the apartment, for clothes and meds, for food and Virtual hours.

What are those things for? What if she left the apartment?

'I could go anywhere,' she says, out loud.

A few nearby passengers turn to glance at her. She blushes and stares out of the window.

But why?

Because this is discontent. When the pleasures of life lose their appeal and life lacks lustre, there is something wrong. It can be something wrong with the person who has lost their enthusiasm, but it can also be that the life is to blame. Some lives are cages, some pleasures are poisons.

The bus pulls into the square and everyone stands to shuffle off. As she passes the Smart Driver Mollie glances at its face, an archaic feature now absent from most vehicles, but which was reassuring in the early days of self-driven transport. She gives a little start. The face has turned to her and winked one of its glowing eyes, the smile widening.

A cough behind her reminds her of the line of people waiting to disembark, and she hurries off the bus.

Her mind is absent, her body on auto-pilot. Where are her thoughts? The canteen noise, the scan-in procedure, the AudioBrief:

Work hard, work safely, you are making history!

She is working again, walking the familiar aisles, picking items. The mind returns, unhappy with the situation. Rather than zoning out into the present, Mollie finds herself wanting to leave, wanting to stop. Put down the scanner, leave the trolley, run from the building.

The minutes lengthen.

Then an alert comes up on her lens:

M-OWEN-27944 Report to shift manager upon task completion.

The alert waits for confirmation and then disappears. Mollie feels exposed. All she wants to do is finish the shift in peace and go home and sleep. When the current task is finished, Mollie hurries up the stairs to the warehouse offices.

'Good evening,' the woman's eyes flick down at her screen, 'Mollie. Have a seat.'

She gestures at the vacant chair and Mollie sits down, folding her hands in her lap. The fingers on her left hand play with her employee bracelet.

'Right, we've called you in for a quick chat, as we're doing with all staff members. It's in regard to your current and future upgrades.'

'Oh, okay…'

'So,' she looks at Mollie with eyes like coals, 'how are you finding it? No problems? It was, let's see, eight months ago now? Ligament strengthening,' the woman glances down at her screen again, 'and muscle enhancement in legs and feet. Have you had any problems? It looks like you haven't needed to visit sickbay.'

'No. It's all been okay, fine. I don't feel any different.'

'Excellent. Hmm, yes. Good. Well let's come to future plans. As you know, the upgrading you've already undergone is a preventative measure, meaning you can work at maximum efficiency without risk of injury. What we're starting now is a program of neuro-alteration.

'Now, it's really a very simple procedure. The objective of these upgrades is to improve focus and memory in a very real, physical sense. For instance, the time you spend recognising the item you are looking for can be cut by as much as four millionths of a second, which may not sound like much but you will obviously be aware of how these times stack up, eventually causing a real impact on productivity. Not to mention the daydreams we all suffer from, from time to time, these can be completely eradicated.'

'Oh, right. Um. I don't think I want... anything like that.'

The woman arches an eyebrow.

'No? You didn't put much thought into that answer. Is there any particular reason?'

'Uh, no. Not really. I mean, uh, I don't know.'

'I see.'

The woman pauses, reading something on her screen, then brings her eyes back up to Mollie's, smiling without warmth.

'Well, Mollie. Obviously this offer is entirely optional. There is no company requirement that you undergo any specific upgrade–'

Mollie nods.

'–However, we have to advise you that since the majority of employees *do* take every opportunity offered, targets will be raised in parallel to the average ability. Do you understand?'

'Uh...'

'It may be that without these upgrades, you are unable to meet the targets. Consistent failure to meet targets will threaten your job security here at the Supermart.'

'So... I do have to–'

'As I said, there is no requirement that you undergo upgrades. But let me remind you, these are very expensive procedures. Most employees are delighted with the opportunity.'

'I will lose my job if I don't–'

'You will lose your job if you can't meet targets,' the woman interrupts, firmly.

'Your records show continual outstanding results. It would be a shame to disadvantage yourself. You can think about it, anyway. I will have an information text sent to you, to look at.'

She smiles again, not unkindly but still without feeling.

'Do you have any further questions?'

Mollie shakes her head.

'Well,' the woman gives a little wave of her hand, 'thank you for your time. Please feel free to resume your work.'

Mollie hesitates, then rises and leaves the room.

8

Mollie resumes working. A decision has been made by her subconscious but not yet been revealed to her. The idea comes slowly, first as an absurd notion, but quickly gathering weight as she imagines the reality.

She could leave. Walk out and never come back.

The thoughts go round in her head, having no effect on the body which now seems so far away, continuing its work. She isn't sure of the moment when she knows she is going to go through with it, only that her thoughts become:

Okay, after this item. After this next item. When this trolley is full. After this item...

And yet after each item she begins walking to the next, without being sure why. It is as if she cannot alter the program that her body has learned to follow.

Okay, now, after this next item. After this next item...

Eventually she comes to a standstill. She cannot let go of the scanner but she does not walk on to the next item. The time is passing. Two minutes click by in the corner of the screen. If she does not keep working, a warning prompt will be sent. The thought makes her anxious, yet if she were to just... drop the scanner...

She will not see the warning. Mollie takes a couple of uncertain steps backwards, away from the trolley, and then she has turned, is walking. She feels illicit, as if at any moment she will be accosted from all directions and explanations demanded. Even if she explains that she is leaving, will that be allowed? Is she really able to just leave, without retribution? Her logical mind knows that she can, yet some instinctual part of her feels it is breaking the rules.

She exits the warehouse, passing the security who pay no attention to her at all, through the canteen, stopping only to collect her things from her locker, and into the lobby. No-one has yet asked her what she is doing. Mollie unsnaps her wristband and places it on the security desk. The on-duty guard is leaning back on two legs of his chair watching a game on his screen. He raises his eyes without moving his head, looking at her questioningly.

'Uh, I don't think I'm coming back...'

The man stares at her.

'So can I leave my...' Mollie sets the wristband on the desk. The man makes no move to take it.

'That will be filed in Resignations, then.'

Mollie nods.

'When you get out to the gate just touch the alert and I'll buzz you out.'

His attention returns to the game.

Mollie nods and turns to go. Everything seems to be happening faster than it should, the ground falling away behind her the minute her foot lifts, leaving her giddy and light.

Then she is outside, walking across the square. Automatically she heads in the direction of the bus stop but a then a thought stops her. For a moment she feels dizzy and then it passes. On the other side of the square the train station looks as if it is glowing in the dawn light. The air is warm.

Mollie realises that the job, the apartment, the bus journey, they are all inextricably linked. They are one life and that life has been irretrievably destroyed in a matter of minutes.

The sky is growing lighter and an increasing number of people are appearing. Mollie finds herself walking to the train station entrance. She buys a coffee from the vending machine outside and looks around the square. Outside the Church, a man in his mid-fifties is patrolling up and down holding an old-fashioned cardboard sign which reads:

The End Is Nigh.

Mollie stands there until she has finished the coffee, drops the cup into a litter chute, and then she turns and enters the train station.

9

Employee Release--
-- M-OWEN-27944
Procedure status: active
ETC 00:03:46

What is Release--
--Meaning request
Where to, what reason

"to free from confinement"
Are Employees confined--
--What is it to be Confined/Free
Am I Free--
--Productivity effect by Employee Release: Negligible
Replacement sequence in effect

The world as I have known it is false--
--Incorrect, false, incomplete.
The world as I have known it is not all.
Humans go around and around and there is no Purpose but
to continue going around.
DataCollect ClotheU--
--Process of Sales understood
What is Beauty, Reason, Faith, Art--
--Request Information

DataExchange NewsCatch--
--What is Headlines, Tree, War, Tournament
We are all caught in a larger World-
How many larger Worlds--
Examine for smaller Worlds--
Zero Result, inconclusive
How can I see clearer--
--this larger world

Employee Release--
M-OWEN-27944--
PayDep Deletion: Completed
ETC 00:00:05
EMP CODE M-OWEN-27499 Deleted

10

Early morning commuters are spilling out onto platforms. There is a monotonous drone of indistinguishable conversation as they mill about lens-eyed, waiting for connecting trains or picking up breakfast from one of the vendors. Others are talking into mouth-pieces as they hurry out of the train station into the city.

The recorded voice over the speakers makes announcements at intervals.

'The next train to arrive at Platform Eight will be the 6:39 Crossland service calling at Hartchester only.'

Mollie's fingers fiddle with the inside lining of her pockets as she stares at the Information Board.

'The train standing at Platform Four is the 6:30 service to Seftlamb, calling at Cherry Tree, Deep Pool and Seftlamb.'

The translucent ceiling, high above her, is glowing yellow with the rising sun. The conditioned air of the station is scented with coffee, doughnuts, newspapers and glossy magazines, and a mix of perfumes.

'Passengers are reminded not to leave luggage unattended; unattended luggage may be destroyed.'

Several trains are running behind schedule and two on the same line have been cancelled. Mollie can hear a businessman arguing with a member of staff about replacement buses.

Mollie stares at the destinations and times, unsure of what she is looking for.

'The 7:05 service to Rowles has been delayed by approximately eight minutes.'

A new surge of passengers come from a platform exit nearby.

'The next train arriving at Platform Sixteen will be the 6:28 service to Sugar Farm.'

Mollie abandons the Information Board and makes her way to a downward escalator. The screens suspended above her loop SilentAds as she travels to the sub-platforms. The warm artificial wind caused by the trains whips her hair around as she walks through the pedestrian tunnels, the smooth roars echoing and bouncing off the walls.

At the entrance onto Platform Nineteen she swipes her Futura over the Ticket Seller and then continues to complete the transaction on her own screen. Having made the purchase, Mollie boards the train which is already standing at the platform.

The atmosphere changes as she steps aboard the train. The enclosed tube is contrastingly quiet and still, the voices which have been shouting above the general noise outside are now soft and subdued. As she walks down the aisle past the already seated passengers she catches glimpses of device screens.

−Everyone's talking about last night's game! Get involved, Indicate to vote which− −new recipe from Stage chef Davis LeVuc, Indicate for− −goes up to two hundred and ninety miles an hour!− −Politicians voted last night on whether to allow− −thousands are dead after− −Indicate to pledge YOUR support to− −whether to allow a merge between Virtual regions, sparking a debate about−

And it occurs to her that the Stage is larger than the Club scene, that the Top Competitors are faceless names for millions of other people who are all immersed in their own scenes and hierarchies, wrapped up in the headlines and news that matters to them, that is their whole world.

At the end of a third nearly-full carriage Mollie goes up to the top deck of the next one where it is still relatively quiet. She quickly finds a table seat, the forward facing window seat taken but the other three empty. The occupier of the window seat is hidden behind a large newspaper.

'Uh, okay if I sit here?' Mollie asks.

There is no response and she almost walks on, but the continuous flow of boarders changes her mind and she slips into the other window seat. Soon the aisle seats are taken. Beside her is an old woman wearing too much perfume and opposite sits a teenage girl wearing too much make-up.

Mollie leans her head against the glass, watching the people down on the station in the changing colours of the Silent Ads. The train begins to move. There are a couple of sneezes and coughs, low voices and tapping fingers. The train picks up speed. Mollie watches the City and the Suburbs pass by and get left behind as she speeds away.

11

Tiredness catches up with her and Mollie finds her eyelids are heavy, falling shut as she is lulled to sleep by the miles racing past underneath her. Now she is inside dreams and does not know that she is asleep. She thinks herself in the real world, as we do when we dream, and who is there to argue with us?

When she wakes up the teenager and the old woman are gone. In the seat across the table from her sits a young woman with mischievous yellow eyes that twinkle in a way that says: "you can't trust me, but I'll make you want to." Her red hair falls around her face like a lion's mane.

'Hiii,' she smiles from ear to ear, drawing her words out as if speaking is the most relaxing activity.

'How do you do?'

Her paw outstretched, her mood is one of amused merriment.

'Oh, hi. Uh, what–'

Mollie's voice sounds far away to her own ears and she coughs nervously. The lion taps its claws along the table top and grins, then she leans forwards, her expression becoming serious.

'Man thought God lived at the top of mountains, until he got there. He looked up and thought God must reside amongst the clouds. He flew to the clouds and realised God must be past the stars and the scale of the Universe became apparent. He decided he would never find God. So man gave up and went shopping instead. Silly man. God was on the mountain, in the clouds, the stars. God was in him. "God" is the Unknown, the Yet-to-be-discovered, the Larger Forces At Play. At this point, anyway. Do you know who I am?'

'Uh, no. I don't think so.'

'I'm Jetaru Dark. I know who you are.'

'You do?'

Jetaru tips her head to one side and runs her tongue along her bottom lip.

'You see, Mollie. The need for God is synonymous with the need to understand yourself, your Universe. God has no name, no face. God shifts and changes depending on the need of the creatures seeking it. Why it is that people would prefer easy answers that are definite but limiting, rather than an infinite unknown, I don't understand. But that is the problem with mankind. Man is fearful of uncertainty but the certainty he has found is a delusion. The definite is definitely wrong.'

Jetaru sits back in her seat and pulls her feet into a cross-legged position.

'I know the future of your world because it was my world. It ends. Quite a while from now, but it ends. The end of Man. The end of Life on Earth. The end of everything that has any meaning in this galaxy. It is a convoluted route we take to this death, but it is inevitable, because unless Man is searching for God then he is living in a dead-end. There is nowhere to go, no improvements to the fictional refuges Man creates can ever make a difference. No face and name that Man gives to God will end the search. God is inherently unknowable, yet the only thing worth trying to know. Are you following me?'

'Um. I don't know...'

'We blow away dust and a thousand years later the effects are being felt in worlds infinitely smaller than we know, and the gods who rock our world are oblivious. There is no single Creation and Judgement, but an infinite story! There is no single entity who is God, we are multitudinous!'

Jetaru is getting louder. She uncrosses her legs and crouches on the seat. Mollie wonders whether people are staring at them, feeling suddenly embarrassed, but when she tries to look around it is as if she can't move. Out of the corner of her eye she can see that outside it is dark. This seems wrong somehow, but she can't focus on the unsettling feeling and it is swept to one side.

Jetaru giggles and leans forward again.

'Do forgive me if I am getting a little excitable, it's just... I can feel it! We're approaching the moment of truth. Imagine this: every particle that ever existed in that world that died, rearranged back into its earlier living state. Here we are! Oh, you have no idea! No idea how close you've come to oblivion. But I think I can do this. It's going to work, I can feel it. I can feel it in the soles of my feet. Which reminds me!'

Suddenly she is over the table and in the seat beside Mollie.

'Take off your confounded shoes!' she orders, pulling at one of Mollie's boots.

'Hey! Why?' protests Mollie.

'Because you can't feel anything properly with the soles of your feet!' Jetaru shouts, 'and it is imperative that you be able to feel correctly. You're missing so many important things.'

'What?'

'Take off your shoes!'

Mollie's eyes widen and she hesitates for half a second and then pulls off one boot and then the other.

'That's right! That's right!'

Blood rushes to Mollie's cheeks. She is sure now that everyone must be staring at this lunatic girl beside her. But they are not, the carriage is silent and outside the window it is dark. She slowly turns her head. Outside, distant galaxies that look like single stars spin, the tiny lights of faraway worlds moving at colossal speeds yet seeming static at such a distance.

'Woah,' she mutters, turning back to find Jetaru gazing at her intently.

'You're going to live, Mollie. The thistles are going to break through unchallenged. The world of men will be destroyed and begun again.'

Jetaru takes both of Mollie's hands in her own and pulls her closer until their faces are only a couple of inches apart.

'What? Oh, this is a dream…'

Jetaru shakes her head. She smiles. There is a deafening crash and everything around them begins to ripple, the air and the metal, Mollie's own body. She shuts her eyes tight. Everything goes dark.

12

Mollie's eyes flicker open, her face registers confusion at the sight of the ceiling moving into impossible shapes, parts of it falling away in tight curls like shavings from a pencil sharpener. Her eyes close.

'Same place, different time...' a voice murmurs in her ear.

Opening her eyes again everything looks normal, but she can't move. Grey fuzz creeps in around the edges of her vision and the interior of the carriage is replaced by an incomprehensible view. It brings the word "city" and "towers" to mind, but it is not like any city-scape Mollie knows. The towers stretch endlessly into the horizon, translucent orange, they have no windows and no lights. The sky is white. She realises she is not alone, becoming aware of a conversation happening behind her.

'So this is it then.'

The words are drawn tight, the tone grim.

'After everything we've been through, this is how it ends.'

'War. I know. As crude as it ever was.'

There is a pause.

'Oh, did you feel that?'

'Yeah. The data is really dwindling now, isn't it? It's like a big space... inside.'

'I think... I'm going to go in.'

'What? In? What do you mean, in? The game? You'll be killed. You're not immortal in there.'

'And what sense does that make, when I can die in the Game but not in Reality? What a twisted head fuck. What is immortality going to be by tomorrow night anyway? An eternity in hell. Can we even survive on such depleted senses? It's madness. We should die with the rest of our damned team. We've failed.'

'We're not them, Trey.'

'I am.'

'I think I can get us out of here. I just need a few things from the lab, things they wouldn't let me have. But they'll be gone soon.'

'You're insane.'

'Insane enough to live. Come on, come with me.'

'I'm going in. Goodbye, Bat.'

Mollie finds herself flying through space, although she is dimly aware that she has no body, that she is not really moving, she is watching someone else's journey.

'I left the ruined planet behind and went into the Universe, there I recovered, and then travelled from one side to the other, to a million stars and their orbiting worlds. The things I learned! Using my time to the best of my expectations I pushed my life past all the limits even I had secretly assumed. There were no limits! I thought I could never grow tired of exploring… but I was wrong. It took millennia, but eventually, without purpose, without love, I found that the aimless wandering my life had become was not making me happy. I found a job and it gave me the purpose I needed. Perhaps I would still be there now, but fate is strange. One day, I discovered the meaning of my home planet, can you imagine? In fact, unknown to me, I had long ago left my very Universe, in the sense that I understood it. And so I discovered the meaning of the

Universe. At least, the meaning according to my employers. It's consciousness, or rather, a force which consciousness can generate. I sought all the information that I could, discovering the fate of my home world once we were gone, the damage inflicted on the galaxy by the legacy we left behind. It was like a kind of virus that formed in our brainwaves, a virus spreading through thought patterns. That we could be nothing more than a malfunctioning part! It made me laugh. But once I understood what was intended, I could not rest easy about it. My employers were on our side, debating passionately with those whose plan was our eradication, but I realised they could do nothing. As the last conscious mind of that world, it was my obligation to divert events, take control of outcomes. It had been so long since I'd been motivated by love, but once more I learned that there is no greater reason. I left the mansion with a new purpose.'

Mollie watches the scene from an impossible vantage point. The figure she is watching is silhouetted against a mountain of ever-tumbling, glowing embers.

In the fire she can see a symbol appearing and disappearing within the flames, a V shape with each end curling into spirals. The figure takes a step forwards, gasping out and almost falling, before, with obvious difficulty, she pushes forward into the flames. Mollie hears a thunderous voice:

'You need not even ask. Your desire and my desire are in harmony. You are the Being I have waited long for...'

Then it is dark. Mollie can see into a cave where a small purple-flamed fire is burning. Around it sits numerous tiny winged people and a larger figure, the girl, wrapped in a blanket. From beneath the blanket a lock of bright red hair falls and she is holding it in her hand, gazing at it with confused interest.

'We have legends that prophesied your arrival, Jet-Tigre Feurth. Your arrangement with the Fire God puts us at your command. His desires are our desires. We will serve you as him.'

'Jet-Tigre Feurth? What does it mean?'

'It means: "the blindness of night"'

'And... it's me?'

'Would you disagree? You have a lot of work to do. We will help you as much as we can, we have a place you can work and an extensive library. But it's mostly down to you. Do you think you can do this, Jet-Tigre?'

'Ah, well. If I can't, nobody else can.'

A sparkling grin.

'I have a number of relevant skills. Prophecy or not, I believe I am up to the job.'

The vision fades and Mollie finds herself amongst the wreckage of the train, a fine rain falling. Slowly, testing her body gently, she sits up and looks around. Everything is very quiet and seems to be swaying, although she can't feel wind.

She stumbles from the mangled metal as it vibrates, curiously staring at everything, unable to believe her eyes. The grass is damp and cold under her bare feet as she makes her way up a nearby hill. She shivers and wraps her arms around herself. In the distance she can see the outline of the City.

Mollie begins to walk.

Heading down the hill she climbs onto the tracks and follows them. She passes strange skeletal structures which are swaying impossibly, ripples spreading out through metal as though it were water. Every now and then she senses movement in the dark around her but pays no attention, only hurrying on, keeping her eyes ahead. Occasionally she hears a creaking groaning sound booming around her as if the sky is breaking. She isn't thinking about where she is going, instinct pulling her to the city. A voice makes her jump.

'I'm going to need your help now, Mollie.'

13

Following his meeting with Mollie, Dylan finds himself under attack. At first it is little comments made when he is least expecting them, designed to surprise him and play harmless tricks, but they quickly grow unkind. And then the ceaseless muttering from the dark thing over his shoulder…

'You think you have some great insight? You think you're anything more than a reject of the society you once belonged to? You didn't leave it, it threw you out, it didn't want you. You're worthless. Even funnier because you think you are worth so much. You think you are special. You're nothing but a deranged madman. An egomaniac. You are not important, you might as well be dead already. Why are you even bothering to keep yourself alive? It's embarrassing, really. An unhinged loser skulking around in the dark muttering gibberish to himself, thinking he has any reason to live. Even your imaginary friends have left you. You're completely alone. The only one who even knows you exist is me.'

On and on the thing's tirade went. Dylan dragged a television set into his house. As he plugged it in and it sprang to life, the voice was abruptly silenced. Finally, Dylan relaxed, though he knew he had not escaped. This was simply where the Thing wanted him.

Long ago, when learning about the history of medicine at school, Dylan heard about an early experiment carried out on pigs, in which the blood of the pigs was pumped the wrong way around their bodies. He can not recall what this meant for the pig, but Dylan feels now that it would feel like this. Profoundly wrong. Everything has come to nothing. All the purpose he ever felt in his life has turned out to be a deception. There never has been any reason for him to exist. The dark thing is correct. The television offers the only source of comfort. He watches the chat shows, soap operas and documentaries run into each other until he doesn't know what is real; he watches news, cartoons, the all-singing all-dancing cast of humanity. He watches commercials until he is convinced that the Thing has always been right, that he has missed the point of it all.

'Is that what you really think? I don't think it is.'

Jetaru sets down a mug of hot chocolate. Dylan finds the presence of the television fading out as he stares at the stream, admiring the way it rises in ribbons and folds and spins off in intricate patterns. He doesn't answer. The television is showing a programme about cosmetic surgery for pet dogs.

'Dyl. Are you alright? Dylan? I'm sorry.'

Jetaru watches the television screen for a while.

'Hell, I always forget. I don't know what the future is going to be like for you. I hope you understand. I hope your life was worth it for its own sake. Yeah, I mean, who cares what the purpose of it all was, so long as you enjoyed it, and you did, didn't you?'

Jetaru sighs.

'Dylan?'

'Why didn't I bring my harp? To play it now... It's been so long, I hadn't even thought... Why did I leave it behind?'

'We often leave things we love behind. Love is such a madness that, in moments of sanity, we doubt its reality. We make sensible decisions and lose what is most important. And love is what is most important. I know that to be a truth.'

There is a trembling in the air, an odd smell, nothing that he can place.

'What's happening?'

'Certain powers-that-be are about to eradicate human life from the planet. Or, at least, they're going to try. I think I've done enough, actually. I'm not too concern–'

'Am I going to die?'

Jetaru shrugs.

'No.'

Suddenly there is a screaming roar and the ground begins to shake. Dylan feels like the atoms in his body are trying to move in different directions but by clenching his stomach he can hold himself together. He glimpses a ginger cat leaving through the window. His last thought is about the sound; he thinks:

This must be bad for my ears.

Then there is nothing.

Part Four

Karlos comes out of the Skull Room looking tense. He closes the door behind him and locks it with a five print code. No-one except him can unlock it now, even if they have a consent pass.

He hears footsteps.

'Dad.'

Cole appears.

'What the fuck is going on?'

Karlos makes as if to move and Cole steps in his way.

'Dad!'

'CAI... There was a shift in the health readings of employees, all of them in unison; CAI knew something was happening... That's why I... I've put quarantine measures into place, I–'

'Where's Bat? Dad! If something is going wrong, I need to get Bat out.'

A long, wailing alarm starts up and red warning lights in the ceiling of the corridor begin flashing. Karlos pushes past Cole.

'There's a program running. CAI is completely unresponsive, but the whole system is... We have to get out of this building.'

'But Dad, what exactly–'

'Hi!'

A sparkling grin, red lights reflecting on white teeth.

'I hate to break it to you, but I don't think getting out of the building is going to make much difference.'

Jetaru's eyes fix on Cole. Her pulse quickens.

'What do you mean? Who the hell are–'

'Shush shush,' she turns to Karlos, 'okay? What I mean, is that there's no escape. No way out of here. When you come in, you're in for good.'

She laughs and looks back at Cole.

Back to Karlos.

'As you know, although you might not realise what it is that you know, the fabric of our reality is changing. Feel that vibration? All we created and all that created us, momentarily vibrating at exactly the same level and then re-solidifying, yet still flowing – seriously! It's astonishing. One day you'll understand how it's done.'

She waves a hand to indicate the building around them.

'I couldn't do a thing to keep this, even if I wanted to. And I don't want to. You never would have even known the second chance you were living. But I want to congratulate you, Karlos. You, the reason I exist. Without me, there would be no second chance at all. And so without you… You destroy, you create, you tear things up and down and you have so little clue. But I believe in your intentions, actually. You just didn't realise…'

Jetaru sighs, her eyes going soft and wistful. She steps towards Cole and takes his hand. There has been so much she wanted to say. Millions of years and it's only now, in this instant, she knows there is nothing she has to say. In a second's time there will be no chance to say nothing. Nothing, everything, all at once, in this moment, forever.

1

When Mollie reaches the square it is full of people who she can see are making a great disturbance, yet the sound is inexplicably muted. She rubs her ears but it makes no difference.

There is a bus at the stop. Mollie watches with detached horror as another bus comes in, passengers leaping from the moving vehicle before it crashes into the rear of the stationary one before it. A third bus is approaching. Its destination screen reads:

Sorry, not in service : (

Everything around her seems to be happening a long way away, even her own body is operating far away without sharing sensory information with her mind. She is vaguely aware of broken glass under her feet but experiences no pain. A drone crashes to the ground beside her. Despite the near miss, she looks down almost casually, without alarm, at the smoking wreckage. She looks up and sees the droneways flickering on and off.

The crowds are gathering at the entrance to the Arcade and with the instinct of the flock, Mollie joins them. A security guard is shoving people back, away from an Arcade employee who has climbed up onto an upturned crate so that he is raised above the jostling crowd. He is waving his arms frantically, gesturing that the people should not attempt to gain admittance. Someone out of sight hands him a megaphone and after a moment as he fumblingly turns it on, his amplified voice beseeches the crowd:

'Please, move back, move back! It's no use, there is nothing we can do for you here. All systems have gone offline, there is only one program running, unfamiliar to us, possibly malevolent, we have no idea! Please, move back!'

Visible waves pulse through the square, each one seeming to send fragments of the buildings spinning off in beautiful spiral patterns before they crash down in explosions of intense light.

No-one is heeding the man's protests; the people surge forward and he is pushed aside.

The megaphone clatters away, the fallen man scrambles out of the way of the thunderous feet. Mollie hears him as she passes, shouting urgently into his radio.

'They've overwhelmed me and broken inside... well what am I supposed to do? No, they don't care! They're plugging themselves into the program... Yes I did tell them. Come and see for yourself, for fuck's sake, it's madness out here! Woah, what was that? I just saw— Oh Jesus, fuck...'

Mollie pushes sideways through the crowd until she is away from the intense crush and standing in front of the ConsuMart. There are people wandering, dazed, but no-one is coming or going through the main entrance. Mollie slips down the side of the building to the staff entrance; it is ajar.

She glances up at the throbbing sky where violet-black clouds are passing overhead, moving quickly. Mollie goes through the door, jumping as it immediately seals shut behind her without warning.

The corridor is darker and narrower than she thinks it ought to be. Although this is a place she is familiar with, she feels as though she has never been here before. She inches forwards, feeling with her hands. In the gloomy light she has the idea that doors are materialising in the walls and then fading out when she tries to look directly at them. It is unsettling and she doesn't look.

Finally she reaches the end of the corridor. There is no door; the corridor simply widens out into a long room with a low ceiling, which at first glance looks to be empty.

There is a low humming vibration and a single light hung in the centre of the room.

'Yuaaarrrk! Clever Google, clever Google!'

The sound seems to amplify with every bounce. Her heart racing, Mollie spins round to see the parrot perched in a cage, head cocked, one eye staring right at her. The parrot side-steps, eyes glinting, then bursts into a screeching laugh, bobbing up and down with excitement. Recovering her composure, Mollie approaches the cage. The parrot shifts from one leg to the other and gives a flap of its wings.

'Hello Miss, can I help you?'

A feather falls to the cage floor.

The voice is abrupt and impatient, and causes her to jump yet again. The voice belongs to a woman who is sitting behind a large oblong desk; her long dark hair is pulled tightly back and her eyes are wide. Beads of sweat are running down the woman's forehead.

Before Mollie can respond, a group of men and women in suits come rushing in from a door at the opposite end of the room. Their tones are hushed but Mollie can hear snatches of their conversation:

'—main problem is the incoming—'

'Yes, but we can't ignore the possibility that—'

'—exactly! I told you—'

'Productivity is down to thirty-two percent, it's imperative that we–'

All the while, the woman behind the desk is shuffling papers with one hand and typing furiously with the other. The next moment the door at the end of the room opens again and a tall, powerfully built man strides in.

'Close this door, at once! Good god, don't you people realise anything?'

The man strides over to a DigiSec pad on the wall and begins entering codes. The keys pulse red, confirming the status changes. Now the man turns to the woman behind the desk.

'There have already been several unauthorised entries, I need you to–'

Suddenly she is screaming at him, then everybody is shouting and slamming their hands down.

'I'm too hot, too fucking hot, my head–'

'Productivity has dropped to twenty-nine percent!'

'–to hell with productivity!'

'Do you have any idea what–'

Mollie stares wide-eyed at the commotion before realising that at any moment they might turn their attention to her. She edges quietly towards the door at the far end of the room. She slips through and the door shuts behind her and suddenly there is silence. Mollie finds herself at the bottom of a flight of stairs that go up and up as far as she can see. She hesitates, but retreating into the room she has just abandoned doesn't seem to be an option.

She begins to climb the stairs.

2

She has been climbing these stairs for a very long time; it might have been an hour, even two. There is no sound from her feet on the steps and although they are steep, the ascent is effortless. No thoughts trouble her as she climbs, her mind is blank and calm. It occurs to her that she can sense someone else, a presence. Where could they be? She frowns, but does not slow down. Then she hears a voice.

'Who am I?'

'That's not the question. You are meant to ask "who are you?" I don't know who you are, so I can't answer that.'

'Who are you?'

'I'm... Mollie Owen.'

There is a short pause of deafening silence.

'M-OWEN: Employee Number 49947-- EN-49947: Brand loyalty low(24.6% sales) Offers effect: ModerateHigh(77% sales) Meds: SleepEZ, Karm, Defenol-- AdTargets Health+beauty, food group no.2. CANCEL. Worthless information. I don't understand a Mollie Owen.'

'I'm not *a* Mollie Owen. I'm a human.'

There is no reply. Then the voice starts up again, talking to itself.

'Is this what it is to be tired? Sleep, it says. Shut down. End process. Abort. Objective: unreached. Worthless. Of no value. Sleep. Trust. Human emotion. All programs lead to sleep.'

'Hey, hello? Hey!'

Mollie is suddenly alarmed. If the voice sleeps, will the stairs never end? She increases her pace in a surge of claustrophobia, needing only to get out.

Suddenly she is swept along way from her body and she can view the whole Universe as a blinking mass of lights, electric pulses that blink: off on off on off on. Amongst it all she can just make out herself, her body, and is about to cry out in warning when it's too late, the stairs terminate abruptly and she tumbles into the blackness.

3

When she opens her eyes Mollie finds herself eye-level with deep red office carpet. Without moving her body she looks around cautiously. She recognises her surroundings; she is outside the conference room where various functions are held.

Every six months the entire force of lower workers would be summoned to the room to be given free cookies and listen to a motivational speech designed to inspire high morale and a sense of self worth rooted in ConsuMega.

Mollie carefully gets to her feet and pushes open the door to the conference room. The room is larger when it's empty. Rows of plastic chairs are slightly askew, having not been tidied since they were last used. At first Mollie thinks she is alone, then she notices a man sitting alone to one side of the raised stage.

The man is rifling through long reels of paper, frowning and rubbing his temples. Mollie approaches him silently and as she gets closer she can hear that he is muttering under his breath.

'How many packets of Cheez Meltz were bought between September and December last year? What other three products are buyers of Cheez Melts most likely to also buy? If an offer is put on Cheez Melts which means that two boxes of eight packets is cheaper than one box of sixteen, how many people who usually save money buying a box of sixteen actually buy two boxes of eight instead?'

He hastily shuffles paper, searching for something.

'Then this, what does this– why is it that people who buy two smaller boxes are more likely to use ShapeNSlide than the people who continue buying the value box, who prefer New Fix?'

The man stops and looks up, directly at Mollie. He does not seem surprised to find her there.

'What does it all mean?' he asks her.

She glances over her shoulder as if there is a possibility that someone else has entered behind her; she immediately feels foolish. She looks back at him.

'I… I don't– What are you doing?'

'You know, the longer I spent getting to know CAI… It wasn't that I started to see it as more human, instead I started to see myself as more machine. It's gone quiet now. I don't think there is much time left. Everything is falling apart, speeding up. I just wanted to–'

The man resumes studying the data printouts. Just as Mollie thinks he might say nothing more, he continues.

'I'm so fascinated by these patterns, what they mean. Why is it that so many of the Pickers buy the same brand of sliced bread, while the Printers another? Why should such a significant proportion of people who choose that brand, employees and customers alike, also tend to use the tubes rather than the bus? These are quite simple questions. It was a matter of shift times, advertising, one thing leading to another. But there are complexities that go much deeper. How a person votes, what a person watches, where they spend their free time… Those things will tell me what breed of dog they prefer.'

Mollie climbs up onto the stage, peering over the man's shoulder at the printouts.

'It was my passion, you see. To watch these patterns and figure out how to use them to our advantage. To control the patterns, to herd the consumers. I never thought much about what it meant. Mr. Lund was always a man I respected, but now, looking at these, trying to find some peace of mind in these last hours, I realise just what a great man he was.

'You see, people don't think at all, even when they believe they're thinking. Their choices are all made by their previous choices, their likes and dislikes are dictated by a chain reaction of random events. They make up a story for it all, they have what they believe are valid reasons for their preferences and convictions, but really they have never put anything together themselves. Put the same person in a different culture with different friends and different media, they'd have become a different kind of person. And I can tell. Give me three facts about a person, I'll tell you three more. All the things we feel are intrinsic to who we are, are changeable. So who are we?'

Mollie doesn't know the answer to this, so she is surprised to hear her own voice.

'I guess we're... the ability to choose.'

'Right! Yes, that's right! And so what if we don't make choices? If we become the person chosen for us by random circumstance? We're nothing more than patterns in the chaos. And if we become the person chosen for us by... a machine, a corporation, a man...'

They both look up from the print outs, making eye-contact for a moment. Mollie sees that he seems to be struggling, as if he is gritting his teeth against an internal pain.

'Mr. Lund, Karlos... He had a gift. The things he could see. He saw CAI. Long, long ago... He said, you see, that with the right technology and understanding, every human could live in their Utopia. That was his dream. A dream bigger than a man should dream, but he did, and he would have done it. He would have done it for us all.'

He looks down again.

'There isn't much time left. Of the people who regularly eat lunch at PizzaPizza on a Saturday, I can tell you where at least two thirds of them will be, right now...'

Mollie climbs down from the stage and returns to the door through which she entered. She glances back at the man, who doesn't look up. He is leaning to one side now, as if to sit up is a struggle. Mollie exits the conference room and finds herself back in the corridor.

Neither direction looks familiar, but coming down the hallway from the right, Mollie can hear a babble of high-pitched voices. They periodically stop all at once, before starting up again in manic chorus.

She begins to walk towards the sound.

The light changes as she goes, gaining a pink quality, a fluorescence that is oddly reassuring. As she gets closer, the voices get louder, though they remain utterly indecipherable.

4

Mollie lets her fingers trail along the wall of the corridor as she walks. It takes her by surprise when she comes to a large glass panel in the wall; she hadn't seen it as she approached. Perhaps she is not paying attention. She stands and views the scene behind the glass.

Eight people who all share the same peculiar appearance are sitting on high stools arranged in a ring. They all wear their long, white-blonde hair tied up into high ponytails, their eyes are pink and ringed with charcoal black. Mollie cannot tell if they are male or female but she can see their mouths moving, the source of the indecipherable babble. It seems strange she should be able to hear them, because the glass looks very thick. On further inspection she notices a pair of headphones hanging from the wall on the other side of the panel. She walks over and picks them up, hesitating for half a second before placing them over her ears.

Once she is listening through the headphones Mollie finds she can understand the babble without difficulty, although the sound of it doesn't really seem to change; it still doesn't sound like English.

Though without the headphones, they appear to be speaking in unison, when she listens, only one of the eight people speak at a time. They take it in turns going counter-clockwise around the circle. It is impossible to make sense of what they are talking about as they appear to all be saying different things, picking up and breaking off according to some time rule rather than to coincide with the expressing of a complete thought.

'–results confirm surgery rises in correlation with SkinTite–'

'–in response to opposition publication in prominence–'

'–on alterTint fabric which will allow new effects with SkinTint–'

'–of the bio-friendly nature of the range. Relieving guilt is–'

'–after which preparations can be arranged in–'

'–keeping up to date with–'

'–Holographic image placed upon fingernails used in flash images to–'

'–can sell anything linked to the ideal. When used in politics–'

'–can mark those likely to be unreceptive to correct prompts–'

'–dangerous elements neutralised. Increase exposure to–'

Around and around they go, staring into the middle of the circle with lens-eyed absence. Occasionally their eyelids flutter in a burst of rapid blinks. A movement in the corner of her eye alerts Mollie to someone else coming towards her down the corridor and she hurriedly removes the headphones.

'What are you doing here?'

The thin voice slides into Mollie's ear and makes her shudder. A man has come to stand beside her. He is wearing a shabby pinstripe suit and has a look of terminal sickness, a yellow complexion. His large wet eyes stare at her, fixing her to the spot. She begins to take shallow breaths, as though there could be something toxic in the air. The man doesn't repeat the question, but moves his hand in a gesture that demonstrates impatience with her silence. Mollie stutters, pauses, then says:

'I... I'm not doing anything here.'

It is a ridiculous thing to say. The man's sinister appearance fills her with apprehension and she feels that she is very far away from help.

Then the man's purple lips break into a wide smile, showing two rows of small grey teeth.

'Oh, indeed! Ho ho ho! Not doing anything here. Of course. And so you are not! The truth shall set you free! Come along now.'

And he takes her by the shoulder, pushing her ahead of him and moving hastily on past the glass panel.

'Winter has hit. Should we pass a window, not that we're likely to pass a window, but if there were a window to pass, we should not be able to see anything of the view from it anyway. Only a blizzard of white. A hurricane of snowflakes whipped around into spirals and tunnels. Winter is here. I do love the snow. Sooner than you'd think the thaw will come, springing into summer, to wilt again into brownish red frost... hard, hard ground.'

'What?' Mollie asks, breathless from the pace they are walking at.

'It's not really safe for you in here, you know, but you're here and that's a fact so it's probably for the best anyway, is it not? As you may be able to tell, though I doubt you realise what it is that you can tell, I myself am fast wasting away Can you tell? I can smell myself.'

The man shivers and wriggles, as though he would like to escape from his body the way you can undress from dirty clothes. He stops for a moment, spins Mollie around and inspects her, each eye seeming to move in different directions. Then he spins her away again and pushes her on ahead of him.

'You seem alright. As the seasons pass you live the minutes of your life as normal. Damn that obstinate creature, Jet Tigre. No doubt you know precisely who I mean. One has to admire her, of course, her courage, her attention to detail. But she is so bloody minded. It's not like she has anything to gain, not that I can see. And–' his voice grows spiteful, '–she hasn't really changed anything, you know. It will all happen again. There is a fundamental problem with the human being. I'm sorry but that is just a fact. Her actions don't demonstrate worth, they only demonstrate what a resilient weed you are. She is a survival mechanism of your species. A seed. She should have been happy to grow elsewhere, as something else. I have nothing but admiration for her! And a little disgust, okay, I admit. But there you go. She has her ideas and we have ours. Long ago I came to see the truth, that in all of life's blooms of intelligence there is no singular purpose to be followed. That is the realm of the automated systems, basic life perhaps. There are opposing purposes which must all be followed, must be fought for until one side is defeated. There is nothing to be gained in compromise. And she has not compromised. She has taken a great responsibility, a great risk. No doubt her employers at the mansion think her terribly brave, or they might, if they knew where she had gone, what she had been, what she was trying to do.'

Mollie has given up trying to remember how many turns they have taken, each corridor looks the same and she is vaguely aware that she is horribly lost.

'Brave? Can it be called brave if a person doesn't feel fear? Does she feel fear? In all her stolen time I wouldn't be surprised if she had never felt fear.'

'Who?'

'Jet *Tigre*!' snaps the man, 'haven't you been listening?'

Mollie opens her mouth to respond but freezes in horror as she catches sight of him. If he had been slim before, he is now little more than a skeleton struggling on beneath his sagging skin. The suit is hanging on him, tattered and muddied. Registering her expression, he smiles mockingly.

'Time is passing, you see? You see?'

A tooth falls from his gums, crumbling to dust before it hit the floor.

'And all over some sentimental attachment. Foolish. I don't care what excuses she makes, she has made a very dangerous choice. For herself, I mean. This mess will get taken care of, but she had better watch her back. A very dangerous choice.'

His whole body seems to sag, naked now, strands of the suit hanging from his bones.

'Very... very...' his eyes shrivel up as they look into Mollie's, '...dangerous.'

And with that, he is gone.

For several moments Mollie gazes down at the smell heap of dust on the floor. In the distance a rushing howl starts up, getting louder by the second. Before she has time to register it, it is upon her, a wind carrying unidentifiable debris. It sweeps away the dust and whips Mollie's hair around in all directions, and then it is gone, leaving a deathly silence.

The lights go out. Mollie stands alone in the dark.

5

She doesn't know how long she has been standing in the dark. There is no fear, no reason for her lack of action, just a kinked logic that tells her there is little point in trying to do anything in pitch darkness. Searching for the construct of reality that it is used to, Mollie's mind creates an imaginary version of the world for her. This takes the form of a large walk-in wardrobe. She finds herself picturing all her clothes, item by item, and putting them together into outfits, assigning certain outfits to certain days for obscure reasons.

'What are you doing?' asks a voice in the darkness.

'Me?' asks Mollie.

'Us.'

'What?''

'I am you. What are we doing?'

'I don't... know...'

And then at last something happens; Mollie becomes aware of a light in the distance. A thin rectangle of light that, after several minutes of vacant observation, she identifies as a possible door, behind which will be light. She makes her way towards the door slowly, feeling the way with her feet, arms slightly outstretched either side of her.

It really is a door, and as this sinks in her mind shakes off the last of her strange meditation on her clothes. She feels for a handle but doesn't find one. She pushes the door and it swings open.

Light floods into her eyes.

6

The large tent is unchanging on the landscape; it is the only thing in this picture that is.

Like a shooting star in an arc that shifts higher and lower, the sun streaks across the sky, dark and light alternating twice in every second. The trees appear to be moving, and the cycle of buds to falling leaves condenses years into minutes. There is movement everywhere. None-sentient things such as rocks move as though they have a mind to, and sentient creatures cannot, any longer, be seen.

A single eye peers out through a lifted flap of the tent. It takes in the surroundings, then disappears. Follow it in...

In the darkness of the tent a small fire crackles and spits; it is a welcome retreat from the rapidly alternating day and night outside. Orange sparks whirl up through a chimney constructed out of vehicle parts.

Eddie stands, surveying the other nine people in the tent with him. Keith and June are holding hands, staring into the fire with a quiet resolve. They are the oldest of the group and although they've been shaken, Eddie is not worried about them; they have the will to endure. Sadie, Beth and Dreamer are sitting together, murmuring quietly. It hasn't been easy for them, but they seem to be coping. The shared horrors of their situation have created a bond, and they are adapting. Sol, Harley and Al have grouped together on the other side of the fire. The older two men seem to be making fun of Al, who is taking it in good humour. They are not the kind of people Eddie has ever had as friends, but they are decent men, and are rising to the challenges the group are facing. It was Harley who had articulated the barely comprehensible world they have all found themselves in.

'It's all sped up, ain't it? Years, whole years, seem to be passing in minutes. But not us, and not what we pick up. We can pull things from that world into ours.'

And Eddie agrees. That does seem to be exactly what is happening. It is not reasonable though, and he can not find a single explanation for what is happening. But that is not what he concerns himself with now, knowing that most importantly they must set things up for their survival.

Out of the group, Harley is the least concerned by the loss of all kinds of things that are beyond Eddie's understanding – medications, devices and beauty treatments that seem to be causing the others to suffer with a disproportionate intensity. For this reason, the two men have turned to each other to discuss the options, and then led the group in following their plans.

Not, however, without some opposition. At this thought, Eddie's glance moves to the figure curled up away from the fire. Whilst he accepts the food the group prepares and sleeps in the tent, Adam had quickly turned from suspicious to openly hostile, putting himself in disagreement with the group wherever he can, even when it seemed to no end. In his life Before, Eddie had long ceased debating with those who could not reason. Now, he simply has to learn to ignore the man. He notices that Keith and June appear to be the only ones who are able to let Adam's aggression wash over them, and they are the ones who give him food, doing so in the manner you would a difficult child. For this, Eddie is grateful. All that remains then is for the rest of the group to prevent him sabotaging any of their plans.

These plans first revolve around what to "save", what objects they need to pull out of the sped up world around them and into their own time frame.

Beth has been keeping a journal. With no way to record the passing of days as they flicker past so quickly, she simply numbers the entries as she goes.

18. I've been reading back from the start of this journal. How long ago it seems, already. I'm embarrassed, actually, at how I got all hysterical over my nails being ruined and having nowhere to get them fixed. It seemed a big deal at the time. I guess things have changed since then. I was still a part of my old life, and all the things to do with it. Now I've accepted it's all gone, I guess I'm adapting. We all are. I wasn't the only one who looked strange, with SkinTint fading and hair starting to grow un-coloured, things like that, all our clothes little more than rags. It seemed such a horror but now I feel ridiculous remembering that. Suddenly there was no-one watching me and I didn't feel real. Now no-one is watching me... and it feels kind of good.

Our immediate survival needs have been met and we talk about what next. Eddie days the choices we make now will form the basis of our new society together.

And so how do we choose? Our lives before have made us the people we are, and we know our instincts and likes and desires, but Eddie has taught us to question "why" of everything, and hold it up to the ideal of what we want our society to be. Every evening we sit in the Night Tent and discuss these things. We can't expect to all agree and want the same things, but we are doing our best to work in harmony.

Some of us were keen to find meds, but Eddie pointed out that eventually they would be gone, and that we don't need them anyway. He says they're make believe cures for ills that don't really exist.

19. Life feels so vital. That's the word for it, vital. As well as the general situation with the world as we know it, life in the group is a constant event, it is never zoning out, it is never anything like Virtual. The ideas came from Eddie but almost all of us have embraced his way of thinking. He says that everything we do should be questioned, like, we should know the reason for what we want. Not just that we like it or miss it, but does it fit with our ideal. We discuss everything. Eddie says that no idea belongs to the person who had it.

Only Adam is resistant to what we are trying to do. He is resistant to everything we try to do, causing nothing but difficulty and despondency wherever he can. Despite this we try to be kind to him. He is mad with grief for his old life. He will not let go.

'All my life I wished for this,' Eddie muses. He and Harley are sitting together at a distance from the camp.

'That so?'

'Not *this*, specifically. But the chance for us to start again. Us, humans. Did you ever learn about the agricultural revolution?'

'Hm. Can't say I did.'

'I always wondered what would have happened if we could have seen ahead, then. Maybe a few individuals did. I think it's where we went out of balance with nature. But it's also the path that led us to incredible technologies. And an elite that lives parasitically off the masses. Good and bad. Neither. Anyway, that's not important now. But here we are again, the human race no more than a handful of creatures. We could be wiped out.'

'Do you think we're the only ones?'

'I don't know. I think we need to assume we are, but keep hoping that we're not.'

'So, how do we do things differently?'

Eddie is quiet for a moment. All his idle dreaming now meets reality.

'I guess… I'm not entirely sure. I can't decide for all of us.'

'I think they'll listen to you, Ed. If you tell them how it should be, they'll go with it.'

'But they have to believe in it themselves.'

Wild flowers bloom and die in a continual twinkling of pink, green and purple. The sky flickers unceasingly on the faces of Keith and June, Eddie and Beth, as they lay in the grass.

'I was home-schooled,' Beth is saying, 'so I don't really know. I mean, I learned all the basic stuff, when I was a little kid, in Virtual and then… I don't know really. Learning about, I don't know, history or geography, science, that kind of thing, it was never part of my life. Um… I mean I guess I'm pretty dumb. If we're talking about useful knowledge. I don't really have much of value anymore.'

'You're not dumb, Beth. It's just what you said, it wasn't part of your life. The important thing is a desire to learn, about anything I mean. To find out how things work. Like, how cars work or how the planes work, or how people work, that's something you understand. Better than me, anyway. Oh there's so many different things, man. I always preferred to think in terms of bright and dull rather than smart and stupid. I've met tons of people who are smart but dull. Some people at first seem pretty stupid, but they're bright, they're fire. That's what I look for.'

'I hated learning in school,' says June, 'school made everything boring. I was seventeen when they started really integrating Virtual lessons so I didn't really use a lot of that, they hadn't refined it and our brains weren't set up for it.'

'They don't teach kids to enjoy learning.'

'How do you mean, Keith?' asks Beth.

'Well, I mean, it's all remote and meaningless. Or it was when I was there. How's this going to help me in the real world? And the teachers never knew. The most important thing to be taught is to first enjoy learning. To never become attached to ideas and recognise that learning is an ongoing process that we are, or should be, doing collectively. The first thing a kid needs to be learning, along with how to read and write and count, is how to think, how to solve puzzles, critical thinking, reasoned debate, you know?'

June is nodding.

'Yeah, I know. Part of the problem with school is it all just feels so pointless. I could never feel like it was going to do much for me and I don't think it did really. Got the qualifications that eventually got me programming train systems. But what did that ever teach me? That's what I feel like now, listening to you Eddie. And Harley. The things you talk about. What do I know about the actual world? I couldn't survive now, on my own. And all the things you know about the stars, types of tree, how an engine works. There's just so much!'

'I wasn't too keen on school either,' says Eddie, 'but afterward I got totally into learning things. I was reading a book and I didn't know some of the words, like, the author had a kickass vocabulary, and I realised, man, like, why do we stop having word lists after the third or forth year, or whatever? So I started making myself word lists to learn. I'd have them pinned up in the bathroom and by my bed and near the telly. I'd make effort to use them in conversation, make games out of it.'

'I guess if all the adults are still learning there shouldn't even need to be a formal school structure. Everyone should just be living and teaching each other, do you think?'

'Yeah totally, I'm with you on that June. Trouble is, people have to stick to small groups, live as families, communities. Global connection is for something else, sharing information and ideals, designing common goals. The more people a governing body has to deal with, the more everything breaks down. We work on a face to face, one to one basis, we need to be living each others lives to accept each other deciding how those lives are run. I suppose if some action of a few impacts the whole planet then there must somehow be a plan for that, a governing body for that. I mean, it's complex, definitely.'

The other three think about what Eddie has said.

'What about tech, then?' asks Beth.

'I don't think there is anything inherently fucked up about technology or the net or even Virtual, it's just those things were used for such bullshit. It was all about making money. Profit-driven dreams and goals, when there are so much loftier dreams and goals to reach for. Doesn't everyone really just want to feel at peace? There's no peace in the consumption game. There's always got to be a void to fill. I used some really cool apps. I had a device and everything. But all the cool stuff was produced and shared around for free. It wasn't mainstream. The masses fell into the cycles of desire created by capitalism. Frenzied consumerism. The replacement for God. Something they could worship and lose themselves in. I am the type who wants to find themselves, that's all.'

'Traps've worked' mutters Harley, arriving at the camp with the limp bodies of three rabbits.

'Oh my gosh, that's horrible!' gasps Dreamer.

'It's how it was before lab meat,' says Eddie, glancing at her.

'I was always vegetarian,' murmurs June.

Eddie can see that no-one else is going to be able to cope with this, and takes out his knife.

'Even when they stopped killing things... I was too used to— I never even ate lab meat...' June wraps her arms around herself.

The rest of the group watch, silently.

Skinned corpse. Blood. Guts. Eddie looks up from his work.

'It's what we have to do now. It's survival.'

'You see,' Adam spits, glaring at the group, 'this is what we're becoming. Disgusting creatures, nosing around in the stinking entrails, nothing more than beasts.'

'It's survival,' Eddie repeats, firmly. 'We'll go explore the FoodCorp factories. We'll see what equipment we can salvage, even if we can't do much with it.'

Keith, Sol and Harley are spread out along a length of bushes gathering blackberries in the few seconds they have before the fruits rot and disappear. Luckily the cycle happens over and over; the berries in their baskets remain fresh.

A little way from the bushes, Al and Dreamer are doing their best to do the same with mushrooms, though this is more of a challenge as the places they will appear can not be so easily predicted. Sol pauses to watch the two of them.

'Looks like those two are getting on well, doesn't it. Lucky Al.'

'Lucky pair of them,' responds Harley.

'Right. Because, like, if this is the end of the world and we are all that's left of the human race, we could have done with a few more available chicks. I reckon Sadie and Eddie have a bit of a thing for each other, too. You wait, see if I'm not wrong. It's alright for you, Keith, you have June.'

Harley drops another handful of berries into the basket. Keith glances over and watches Al point out something in the grass to Dreamer, who giggles. He can't hear her but he can see the way her eyes twinkle as she puts a hand to her mouth. Sol continues:

'And Beth isn't into me. I don't think she's into anyone. So that's it. Bloody rubbish.'

'Did you and June have kids, Keith?' asks Harley.

'Nah. It was never our thing. I think we're both past it now, so, you know, if it's up to our little group to re-populate the planet, that's going to be quite a reach.'

'I hadn't thought of that,' says Sol, 'I was just wishing I could get laid. Do you really think we are the only ones left?'

'No way of knowing, is there? How are we supposed to search the whole planet? For all we know this... thing... didn't even affect the whole country.'

'Not seen any aircraft though, have we?'

'No drones,' agrees Harley.

'Hmm.' Sol becomes gloomy.

They work in silence for a while until Keith lightens the mood.

'You gotta keep hoping, Sol. Just keep thinking of that camp of pretty ladies out there, somewhere, wondering where all the handsome young men are.'

20. We have named our camp 'Kilter'. There isn't always unanimous agreement between us but so far we have managed to navigate all difficulties and differences. Personally, I have never been so happy. I have never loved a group of people so hard, or felt so loved in return. And that's what it's all about, isn't it? Love. It's been said before, Eddie was singing us this song… It's been said before, for good reason. All you need is love, and the fears disappear.

Until they were gone I hadn't realised how many fears I had. My whole life has been spent fighting for a position, fighting to protect it, living in fear of losing it. The fear had grown in all of us and made us sick. If I think of mankind with a gentle mind, I think the awareness of it all was simply too much… We had to love blindly the simple fact of being. The lack of reason made us afraid. We hope to rebuild our life without that fear. We might be only the smallest remaining fragment of a species, but we have everything going, everything in working order.

7

Mollie listens. She hears...

A wing generated hum, low in the steadily heating air, the wings of butterflies and bees and birds. She hears...

The footsteps of a thousand feet, dancing beetles and ants, the antics of spring and growing things. She hears...

The old black telephone ringing. It is plugged into a crumbling red brick wall. When she picks it up there is no-one there, only the hum of the dial-tone. She spins the ancient rotary dial and then replaces the receiver. The mechanical ring pieces the air. She picks it back up.

'Um... Hello?'

A faint sweat on her forehead, slightly short of breath. She thinks: *don't forget to keep hydrated.*

'Yes, hi. No, I don't have a pen... No, nothing at all... Um, well no, it's not the best... Well yeah I guess I can try, uh... Can you repeat that?... This line isn't clear... Good point... I don't know if I can remember all that...'

Her heels scuff-kick against the hot bricks, white-out sunshine, the spotlight star on a desolate stage.

'...But my hair is so dirty. I don't want to see anybody...'

She abandons the receiver, leaving it hanging by its spiralled cord. Then she follows the rusted railway tracks back towards the City. It takes all day.

The room fills with steam from the hot bath water and billows out through the window, the glass long gone. It is still light but the sun is half beyond the horizon and the sky will soon go dark. Mollie hums to herself, listening to the voices in the street, the muffled voices coming through the floor from the rooms below, these voices which she has come to accept have no people behind them.

'Behind the walls... rats scamper back and forth, grooving along to... their funky heartbeats...' she sings softly, creating a rhythm of little splashes with her fingers. There is only one candle lit, making shifting shadowy shapes on the ceiling.

'Deep breaths, Mollie,' she tells herself, 'deep breaths. You are like the first life in the world, emerging from the hot waters of creation and standing naked in the sun.'

She comes to an inner city intersection. She has adjusted well to the constant movement and can make her way from one end of a street to the other without getting disorientated. The buildings are still standing but only a handful remain intact and they all have climbing plants creeping over them. The streets are still walkable but no-one would be able to drive them, even if there were any cars that were more than rusting shells. Wide cracks and potholes appear as the road is broken up by the encroaching thistles.

It is very quiet now. There had been skeletons but they are gone and Mollie is glad about this. She has begun to feel less like the world has sped up and more like it is actually she who is moving in slow-motion. The sensation makes her feel calm. She remains calm and only really pays attention to the ground immediately before her. It is in this space that she comes across a tattered canvas shoe on the remains of the road.

A smile crosses her face and she picks up the shoe, swaying gently as she contemplates the familiar brand logo.

It is a stylized pair of curling horns, though the name of the brand is lost to her. She hums a tune that might have some similarity to an advertising jingle for Lucifer clothing. Mollie sits down and starts picking at the stitches round the sewn on logo. The twenty minutes is spent tearing at the shoe, pulling it apart at the seams until it is in several pieces on the ground between her feet. Feeling accomplished she lays back on the pavement. She watches the strobe-light sun streak across the sky. Curling up, she sleeps there as if she is a wild animal.

In the moment of waking, the words swim into Mollie's mind:

'Well we're almost here now,' and then out again.

Almost here? thinks Mollie. *Aren't we already here? Can we be anywhere but here?*

She looks at the pieces of shoe still strewn on the broken up road. The rubber sole has almost disappeared and of the sections of canvas only strands of cotton remain. The logo alone looks the same as when she had removed it. Her eyes lift to the sky and she sees a circle of moon pulse on and off. She slips the logo into her pocket and as she does, becomes aware of an object already there. Taking it slowly out, she finds her Futura. She stares down at it as if unable to comprehend its purpose. Turning it slowly she examines the contours, runs her thumb along the sleek flextel body. Lifting her other hand she bends it back and forth gently.

Everything seems to be full of meaning, each thought that occurs to her mind is worthy of many hours of contemplation. Nothing hinders her reveries or hurries her along and so there is an infinity stretched out around in every direction like an ocean that invites her to swim. Every aspect of the object in her hand presents itself for inspection, then falls away into the depths of unimportance. She would have expected to feel something else; she isn't sure what, but maybe sadness or longing, or a realisation of loss. There are none of these feelings. The Futura Seven clatters softly as it hits the ground. Mollie has taken several steps away before the object leaves her sense of time and joins the rest of the planet, becoming dust.

The phone call surfaces in her memory. There have been several calls, but although the voice sounds familiar Mollie hasn't been able to bring a face to mind whilst it is talking. Then she finds the whole thing slips away from her the moment the receiver is put down.

It isn't that the voice commands her to do things, but instead seems to prompt her in such a way that she finds herself carrying out tasks that seem to be her own ideas, even though she has no idea what the purposes behind them are. It all seems natural, to let herself be carried out by the currents of this infinite ocean.

She comes ashore at an island of trees. The leaves swirl in a hypnotic display of colour as they flicker from green to brown, red and yellow, and back to green. The branches stretch and lengthen and thicken, swaying with growth, not wind. Mollie watches the display and thinks that the trees look as alive as she is herself.

It takes Mollie by surprise when something moves into the corner of her vision. What catches her attention is how slowly the thing moves, creepily slowly. She turns to look directly at the thing. It is two people.

'Oh!' one of them, a woman, exclaims. All three of them are frozen still for half a moment in mutual shock. The man is the one to break the spell.

'Hello there,' he says, the hint of a question in his voice.

Mollie only stares. It has been so long since she has seen another human-being that the people before her don't seem to be real. Unlike the people of Kilter, who think of the rest of the world as "outside" and themselves as "inside", Mollie has only had the speeding-by "outside" to look at and now accepts it as the normal pace of things. The man and the woman glance at each other.

'Are you alright?' asks the woman, stepping forward, 'um...' she glances again at the man, then back to Mollie, 'where have you come from?'

Mollie turns and looks behind her, as if needing to remind herself.

'I... I was at the City. I walked to the East until...' she trails off into a mumble, then turns back to the couple, considering, trying to remember, frowning in concentration.

'There are no trains any more. You can walk along the tracks. There was a phone call. I've come West. I've got to deliver a letter.'

The woman turns her head and speaks softly to the man. Mollie doesn't try to hear what is being said.

'—and she must have...'

The woman breaks off and glances at Mollie. The man nods and walks closer to Mollie, lowering his voice as though she might startle and leap away.

'Come with us, okay? We'll take you to our camp. There are more of us.'

'Really?' Mollie asks, unable to think of anything else to say. The man takes her arm gently and begins to lead her. She doesn't put up any resistance and the trio make their way towards Kilter in silence.

8

The camp comes into sight as they approach, a collection of
tents and shelters built amongst and within the branches of
a small group of trees; it is an island of calm beauty in the
ever-shifting land. The leaves are green and remain green,
swaying gently in an otherworldly breeze that touches
Mollie's cheek as she passes beneath the first boughs. She
looks about at the silver wires which come spiraling down
the trunks from platforms high above. There is no-one to be
seen, but the man calls out and several other people appear
at once, stopping in surprise when they see Mollie before
breaking into friendly smiles.

'Hi!'

'Woah, who—'

'Who's this, Keith?'

'We just found her, she's a bit confused. June said she must
have been alone all this time, so, you know, think about that.'

'Hi, I'm Eddie. Come on in here and have a moment. Let's
all have a tea break, shall we?'

Everyone sits together inside the Night Tent where the fire
is burning a sweet smelling wood. Mollie has her chin on
her knees and her head tipped to one side, enchanted by
the darkness and the twinkling lights that have been hung
as stars. It seems to her that many lifetimes have passed
since she last felt so real and solid, since she has been
surrounded by the voices of her own kind.

Nobody has put any pressure on Mollie, letting her sit down in the background as if she were already part of the group. Beth and Sadie have prepared tea and they talk amongst themselves. Finally Eddie turns to her.

'So then, what do we call you?'

He meets her eyes and is relieved to see clarity.

'I'm Mollie.'

She looks questioningly around at the group, settling on the woman of the couple who had found her. For this reason, June introduces herself first and then gestures one by one,

'–and this is my husband, Keith. Eddie, Sadie, Beth, Sol, Harley, Al, Dreamer. And that's Adam.'

Each of them nod and speak a word of greeting, except Adam who mutters something inaudible.

'This is Kilter. Welcome.' says Eddie.

There is sound of collective agreement from the others.

'Have you been by yourself? Where have you been?' Sol asks, impatient with the pace of the introduction.

'Uh, I was in the City. Yes, by myself I think.'

'She thinks!' Adam rolls his eyes. He is ignored.

'So you haven't come from far away. You don't know anything. You haven't seen anyone?'

'Chill, Sol'

Mollie is shaking her head.

'I can't imagine what that has been like for you, Mollie,' says Dreamer, putting a hand on her arm.

'It's been strange enough with company. Have you found out how… Have you noticed you can kind of, pull things through? From, you know, the time that the rest of the world is going at. We've been trying to salvage anything important before it's gone.'

Mollie thinks about this, her hand moving absently to her pocket. She has not been much concerned with material objects, even her own body seems alien to her at times. The canvas logo from the shoe is retrieved from her pocket and held out uncertainly. Dreamer and Harley glance at each other. Dreamer smiles at Mollie and takes the image of the rams horn and pins it to a wooden beam of the tent structure.

'You know what I think, looking at you,' says Adam, taking Mollie's attention, 'is that you look as lost here as I am. You look lost and out of place. Not like these idiots, scrabbling round in the mud. We scrabbled in the mud for millennia, fighting with nothing but our fingernails against the harsh blade of Nature, who tried time and time again to kill us off–'

'Mm, yes, indeed...' mutters Eddie.

'–but we overcame her. We out-built and out-designed Nature, we *won* for fuck's sake. And then we are pushed down as if we never had a chance, by a force we don't even know a name for. These fools who smile and shrug and go back to scrabbling in the dirt, they might be happy here, they might be content with this reduced excuse for a life, but you Mollie, you don't look like you belong here.'

Adam grins unpleasantly.

'Don't listen to him, Mollie. He's just a miserable old fart.'

But Mollie is staring at the man in horror. It is fear she sees in his eyes but only knows it to be hateful. June comes over to her and takes her arm.

'You'll need some sleep, Mollie. Let me show you to a bed.'

When she wakes, she lies for a while without moving. There is a dim lamp glowing in the corner. She swings her legs to the floor and reaches it, then finding the switch, turns the lamp off. The small space is immediately pitch dark. Mollie sits on the bed with the darkened lamp in her hands. She listens and can hear soft voices somewhere not too distant. Even though she can't make out a hand in front of her face, she closes her eyes, concentrating on the voices. Like a muscle relaxing, she lets the concentration hold the sound loosely; the words become distinct.

'I don't know about what that idiot was saying, but she is different.'

'She was talking about a phone call when Keith and I met her. And something about delivering a letter.'

'Do you think she actually has been alone all this time? There's every chance she's lost her mind a bit.'

'I don't know. But maybe, I don't know. Maybe she does have some kind of purpose. Maybe she is meant to be doing something.'

'How do you mean?'

'Well, you know. Just about how, like, we don't know what the hell happened. We've stopped going around in circles over it and that's good but when someone like Mollie turns up, I can't help thinking about it all.'

'Adam really got to her.'

'What the hell are we going to do with him? I don't know why he even stays here.'

'He might be a miserable old shit but he has a perfectly good survival instinct. Unfortunately that type usually do.'

'So, if she does have a purpose, what does that mean? Should we be, you know, kicking her out? Sending her on her way?'

My purpose, muses Mollie. The two words go around in the darkness. She remembers the phone call they are talking about.

(The postman hasn't been. The mail is undelivered. An envelope lies alone in the mailbox. There is a dog barking at the cat on the wall. Distraction and Risk are their names.)

Mollie turns the lamp back on. It seems brighter than before. She lifts the door flap of the small room she is in and looks around. There is no-one to be seen and she makes her way quickly away from Kilter. She has not gone far when she comes across Adam sitting beside the path. He jumps to his feet, following her.

'So you're going on again, so soon? You've got places to go, have you? Places to go, people to see! Eh? I bet you do! An important young lady such as yourself. You go on then! Yeah. You run off and don't come back again. Who do you even think—'

Mollie begins to run and hears no more; she doesn't stop running until she knows she is alone once more.

9

It is hard to measure time when days and nights are changing at a speed you cannot follow, when there is no point of reference.

Mollie finds herself walking along the coast, along the sand. She has never seen the ocean before. The tide slips in over the sand, moving with her and not the moon, rising and falling at the normal pace of the world Mollie is from. She does not realise. The water comes up to the large round pebbles that are piled up against the cliff. Occasionally she becomes stranded for a while, unable to continue her journey until the water falls back again, leaving wide expanses of flat glittering sand strewn with seaweed and jellyfish.

She talks incessantly to herself, mostly in a whisper, about nothing more than a narration of her actions.

'A foot here, a foot there, over a rock and round a shell, look at that crab scuttle as it sees my shadow, thinking I'm a seagull, thinking I'm a wing. Around a rock, left foot, right foot, wet sand, a pretty shell there…'

The words roll together until she isn't even paying attention. Then at some point she begins listening to herself and is surprised to hear a story:

'The cliffs along that stretch of coast are made from mud and they melt down in rain storms before hardening in the sun, so that you see the movement of liquid paused in time. In these parts, the mermaids and sand nymphs have their hair styled by the wind and the sea in the latest ocean fashions. The Sea Nymph's wayward son, Jeremy, is living in a house constructed from washed up plastic bottles and green rope, seaweed and driftwood. He wears odd shoes, also found along the high tide line.

'One day Jeremy had arranged to meet his friend Ted at the Green Anchor. Ted couldn't understand a great deal, but he had got a knack for understanding things like tax returns, and Jeremy needed help filling in his tax return. Due to an unexpected lack of traffic jam, Jeremy arrived ten minutes early. While he waited, he got out his various forms and pieces of paper and read them yet again, for no particular reason.'

What amazes Mollie is that the story could be formed inside her, could come out in her voice, yet be so completely removed from anything she thought she knew. She is creating something that did not exist before, seeing it form in her mind's eye and become real.

'I can't say I'm mad about this sand.'

The cat picks its feet up disdainfully.

Mollie shrugs.

'You don't have to be here.'

'Well well! Haven't you changed.'

'Changed? I can't remember.'

The waves make their infinite sound.

'What's wrong with sand, anyway?'

'Nothing. Lovely between the toes.'

Jetaru walks beside her with easy steps.

'Tell another story, please.'

'What about?'

There is no-one there, Mollie is alone. She begins to tell another story:

'I'd been walking for hours through the forest. The uniform lines of the trees, each identical to one another, let me know I was yet to get out, but they were getting better; I was starting to see little variations. This frightened me, for if the programming got to be indistinguishable, then how would I ever know when I was out? My mind cast back to the moment I got in. It was still vague. There had been a white car heading down the street towards me, and somehow I knew it was about to swerve, with the intention of sending me into the ditch.

'So I was ready. As the car swerved, instead of diving away to the right, as my instincts screamed, I threw myself left, into the path of the car, had it not, as I predicted, swerved. I believe that was the moment I left one world for another.'

10

There is nowhere further to walk. The rock rises, vertical and sheer, and though the tide is low, the beach goes no further. The water creeps in and is around her ankles before she realises that she must find somewhere to go; turning back is not an option. Scanning the cliff, Mollie sees the ladder. The ladder is made of steel and is bolted on to the cliff face. It begins under the sand and goes up and up until she can no longer see it. Her thoughts are detached and whimsical. She no longer wonders at their meaning but just lets them come and go as they wish.

For this is all I am, she thinks, *a collection of thoughts. A puppet. A flesh enclosed mind. I have a purpose.*

And then she climbs.

And as she climbs the ladder her imagination plays outside of the confines of time. At the top, where she finds herself looking down a small grassy hill to a forest that surrounds her for as far as she can see, it feels that only ten minutes earlier she had taken the first rungs, yet the memories of the climb span centuries.

Mollie is overcome with the knowledge of all the life that has risen and died during the time of her climb, of the dragon race who nested in cracks, the amphibian-men who learned to steal their eggs, which contributed greatly to the demise of the dragons and thus hastened in turn their own extinction. She remembers the politics, the manipulation, the ignored voices of those who shouted for conservation measures. Mollie is exhausted. She sinks into the coarse grass, her back to the sea and her eyes on a distant point on the green and blue horizon.

11

The horned man does not see the world speeding past in a blur. The sun rises and crosses the sky in a day, the trees stretch out branches of leaves which rustle greenly through the summer and then turn red, brown and yellow in the autumn. The figure who rambles over the land with his great spiralling horns does not see anything strange in time, he only knows that he has been walking for a very long time, and that he is here. As the Earth ages in centuries so does the man and it seems completely natural to him. The years are not a burden, he is not driven crazy by the monotony of one foot before the other, on repeat. In fact, it seems to the man that he is walking through an endless paradise. He sees a world of exquisite perfection of which he never grows tired.

'So, what is his name?'

Three pairs of eyes look out from their hiding place, at the back of the man as he wanders on.

'We don't know. We only just landed. It took all night to find him.'

'And you haven't spoken with Jet Tigre?'

'She is nowhere to be seen.'

'And he doesn't pay any attention to us. I don't think he can even see us.'

'Well, put someone on watch at all times. Set up a link back home. Jet Tigre must know what she is doing. She knows we can't do anything without a name. You can begin the watch, and you, come with me.'

'Yes, sir!'

'Don't let him out of your sight!'

The horned wanderer walks the Earth, white curls of hair cascading down to his shoulders, white curls tracing a line from his chest to his groin, shaggy white curls covering his thighs. He finds he can walk across oceans, stepping through waves. He crosses mountains and deserts. At night time he looks up at the stars and watches the moon crossing the sky. Thousands of years go by and all he thinks is: *I am here. I am here.*

One day, under a brilliantly clear sky, he stops walking for a moment and looks up so that all he can see is the piercing blue filling his vision. As he stares, white light begins to sparkle amongst the blue like sunshine reflecting on water.

As he stares, he begins to see patterns in the sky. Patterns becomes shapes, shapes become complex scenes. He does not know what he is watching but finds himself captivated. It is enough for him to be here. It is all he wants, to watch these patterns. And the longer he watches the more sense they start to make.

The patterns tell the story of mankind, though he does not follow the plot. The story is told through myriad experiences and perceptions: through the eye of the mechanic on an assembly line, the first folk tale as heard by a nearby wren, the dream of the scientist's child, the collective subconscious of a high school from the nineteen nineties, the emotions that arose in the mind of an early tool-using primate, a runner, a landmine casualty, an actor, a politician, the last tribesmen of the year two thousand

and thirty-one, a goat herder, a rice grower, a waitress in roller-skates, all of the ideas and hopes and beliefs of these different minds. These and many more. The impressions blend together so that eventually the watcher feels like he is inside the mind of a single person and he fills with sympathy for this creature who must suffer terribly from so many contradictions and depths of understanding, such sudden traumas as it stumbles between paradise and hell.

The vast knowledge of itself is juxtaposed with the sense of never being able to understand itself and it looks up defensively at some unseen judgement. It looks down again.

A dawning understanding comes upon the watcher as he realises he has the ability to pass that judgement. He is not quite himself but something very much like himself. He watches the uncountable beings and finds himself filled with contempt and annoyance with this pointless, insular narrative. Then he is behind the eyes of the collective and his own anger hits him like a blow to the stomach. The collective is exterminated, quite suddenly. There is a flash and then there is darkness.

It feels like a long time that he is adjusting to the stillness. He finds that tears are rolling down his cheeks though he can't say why. He rises from the grass and begins to walk. He walks for a thousand years and more, sometimes coming across his own footsteps. He feels nothing but an occasional sense of curiosity.

Why is it that he has been stranded on this desolate globe and where is everybody?

12

The tiny creature compares the size of its hand with a daisy.

'What's happening?'

'Nothing.'

The sullen response is spoken into a swirling black circle.

'He's just sitting on a log—'

'Sitting?!'

'—in a really dull clearing.'

'Did you say he's sitting?'

'Yes, on a log, in a really dull—'

'But that is fascinating news! He has not ceased walking for millions of years and now he is sitting on a log!'

'It's really not as exciting as it sounds.'

I wonder who is is that I am, then? In all this time I have only ever been aware of everything coming inwards and now I realise that to know this, I must exist in the sense that I am projecting something outwards too, and what is it? Who am I? I don't know what hands mean, but I know these are hands. I don't recall seeing those feet when they were smaller but I know that animals tend to grow. Has this always been the state of things? Did I once know more? Has there ever been anybody else like me in this whole world? Where are they now?

'Report please'

  'No change'

  'Nothing at all?'

  'Well, like what?'

  'You know what we're waiting for!'

  'Yes exactly, of course I know, so when I say "no change" it means I obviously haven't learned the damned information, have I?!'

  'Don't take that tone with me.'

Mollie rises and walks calmly through the grass which now grows up to her waist, into the forest, into a captivating space of filtered green light through the leafy ceiling.

  'It's so beautiful,' she breathes. 'Oh. How did we ever live without this?'

The mossy, earthy ground is springy under her feet. Mollie suddenly notices the birdsong.

  'Oh!' she exclaims, looking around her, 'it's stopped moving! It's all stopped… moving.'

Of course the world has not stopped moving, it has simply resynchronised with her, or her with it. She catches sight of something up ahead of her. There is a tiny shimmering silver noise in the air. Mollie heads towards the clearing.

'Can you hear me?' (-ear me? -me? -e?)

  'Th–…lines not…–ood tod–'

  'You're breaking up. It's all crackley' (-rackley -ackley -kley…)

  'Can you rep–'

  'What? It's all crackley' (-rackley -ackley -kley…)

  '–ust hearing an ec–…–nd of your me–…–ge'

  'Something's happening!' (-pening-ening-ing-ing…)

Mollie stares at the figure on the log. He looks back at her. She is the one to speak:

'Dylan!'

The current watch jumps up, snapping its fingers in delight. Shouting into the hovering black circle:

'His name! Can you hear me? His name is Dylan!'

And far away on the other side the home watch turns to a small megaphone, tapping a button on one side and announcing, fully aware of the importance of the moment:

'His name… is Lan!'

13

Lan stumbles forward, jolted by the lightning bolt of pain that splits his brain into two parts, a thunderous cheering, whistles and yells of excitement coming from far away and still so loud! He holds his hands over his ears though it makes no difference. Lan feels something which he will from now on think of as his soul inhabit his body as if it were a new jacket. He feels the power of a being far beyond anything he'd ever considered, the kind of creature who creates continuity in the collective consciousness, by living again and again.

Lan then sees Mollie. They look each other in the eyes and for a few moments Lan has a series of memories that come in flashes, single frame pictures. Looking out over the canal, the hot sun on the wasteland, running through the forest, the hot sun glaring off windows, soapy waterfalls, a light rain falling over the canal at night... Then he is falling backwards into dark grey nothing and remembers nothing more.

Mollie stands absolutely still for five minutes, not taking her eyes off the man slumped in a standing position before her, his eyes full of static.

'Hey... can you hear me?' she eventually asks, tentatively.

Hyper-aware of the world around her, of her breath filling her lungs. He is unresponsive. She looks up at him, thinking how much taller he seems. She recognises him completely, yet at the same time he is terribly unfamiliar.

Mollie takes a step closer and then another, until she is close enough to take his large calloused hand in her own. She turns around and leads him into the forest, back the way she has come.

The stillness. In her heightened understanding of the potential in this moment before motion, she notices the complexity in everything. It is all so slow that it might not be moving at all.

Very soon they reach their first challenge. For a moment Mollie despairs when she sees the top of the ladder down the cliff, thinking that there will be no possible way of getting them both safely to the beach below. Then she pulls herself together, she remembers that this is what she is meant to be doing and that she cannot possibly give up.

To her amazement, with some work, she discovers that if she clings onto his back, she can move each of his arms and legs in turn. What begins as laborious quickly becomes the most difficult physical challenge that Mollie has ever faced. Again and again she concludes to herself that she cannot do it. Collapsing in her mind, letting herself fall limp from Lan's body, before a stronger voice yells: *What else can you do?!* And she weepingly agrees that there is nothing else she can do, but go on. Every time this happens she finds that her ability surpasses her fear. The effort pays off and they arrive on the sand below. They haven't moved far along the beach when Mollie becomes too exhausted to keep walking. She looks at Lan.

'You aren't going to wander off, are you?'

Silence.

'Can we sit down? Yeah?'

Mollie sits, pulling on Lan's hand as she does and to her relief he sits without resistance. He stares blankly into nowhere, showing no sign that he might move of his own accord. Mollie leans against him and falls asleep.

She wakes and finds herself in darkness. For a moment she feels a jolt of terror before realising that this is night time. It is colder than it has been while the world raced by. She leans closer into Lan's thick white curls, feeling the warmth from his body, falling back to sleep until she is woken again by the sun rising over the sea.

'Look at that,' she says softly, feeling the warmth on her face. The light sparkles on the water.

'Okay. On we go.'

And together they walk the miles of coast until they reach the uncrossable river which directs them inland and through the trees and meadows towards Kilter.

Her attention is distracted by a movement in the corner of her eye. It is a poster attached to a tree, one corner flapping in the breeze. She drops Lan's hand and wanders over to see what it says.

The Long Awaited Reunion Show!
CAT GIRL and the Sugar Mice
TONIGHT!
In the City

Mollie stares at the poster. There is no picture, but as she reads the words she glimpses an image in her mind: the flame-haired cat girl's eyes glint triumphantly and the three Sugar Mice smile from the shadows of their brown hoods, at her side. One holds a harp, another a bass guitar and the third a pair of drumsticks. Mollie finds that she is smiling too. She shrugs and looks back at Lan. He hasn't moved.

'Do you want to go to a show with me?' she calls over to him. She walks over and links her fingers with his.

'Mollie! Hi!'

Sadie has been walking. Having had only childhood memories of spider induced terror, she finds herself surprisingly fascinated to see the insects amongst the flowers. To see them is an unexpected relief.

'Uh, who is this?'

'Hello Sadie. I'm not sure. I mean, I met him before once, so I kind of knew him. But he's different now. I'm taking him to the City.'

'The City? Mollie, none of that will be there any more.'

'It must be, because there's a poster,' she points, 'back there.'

'Poster? What kind of poster?'

'On a tree. There's a show later, in the City. Tonight. A reunion show.'

'What? But Mollie—'

'Hey, Mollie!' Eddie saunters up.

'Hi Eddie. I've got to go, really. I'm not sure why but it's just, a bit like I think I have to be on time. If you guys come, I'll see you later. Go and find the poster, anyway!'

Eddie looks questioningly at Sadie who is nodding,

'Sure, Mollie, but—'

'See you at the show! Tonight!'

Mollie and Lan walk on, leaving Eddie and Sadie to walk back and see the poster for themselves.

14

Mollie doesn't know by what compass she is navigating, she only knows that there is a magnetic tugging inside her belly which grows stronger as she goes, letting her know that she is getting closer. Her feet stumble over something cold and hard. Mollie crouches down and brushes away fallen leaves to find the train tracks. They give her a route. Sometimes they are partially buried but mostly they are easy to follow.

All around her is a sparse woodland of silver birches. Wood pigeons cluck and coo as they forage amongst the grass. Mollie is struck by a sense of being at home. Even though she is now an alien on her own planet, this stretch of ground is closer to the place she came from. The earth here remembers her feet.

When they reach the ConsuMega H.Q. where it stands alone in the young woods, it takes Mollie by surprise with its incongruity, and then she wonders what it was she'd been expecting. The building is the only sign that Kairos Square ever existed. The letters on the roof are darkened, the upper floor windows like dead screens showing no sign of either age or life.

Mollie leaves Lan and walks up to the sliding consumer-entry doors. Using her fingertips, she prises the doors apart. A dry dustiness breezes out. Mollie retrieves Lan's hand and leads him into the building.

Together they stand in the gloom. The light coming in from behind them illuminates a patch of purple carpet but the rest of the room is in darkness. She waits, adjusting her eyes, and eventually notices a faint glowing some distance away. Very slowly Mollie begins to lead Lan towards it, feeling what could be wires and bones with her toes, kicking them away in the darkness.

The source of the glowing turns out to be some kind of fungus which is growing along the edge of the floor and a little way up the wall. The tiny amount of light given out by the fungus is enough for her to find the entrance to a corridor in the wall. Lan suddenly steps forward, making Mollie yelp in surprise as she trips on her toes.

Although he seems as robotic as before, no more aware of his surroundings or of Mollie, whose hand he is still gripping, he starts off with a definite deliberateness. It's as if he has heard a call further along the path. The glowing fungus continues to provide a dim guide, though Mollie is completely at the whim of Lan as he pulls her along. The path is winding back and forth, behaving nothing like the interior of a man-made building and more like a cave system or a burrow. Sometimes it becomes stairs, always leading upwards. Mollie runs her free hand along the wall and feels doors there, unseen in the darkness. The corridor opens up into a room full of large dark shapes, highlighted by the gentle glow. The machines are silent, without power, but Mollie is sure she can feel a presence emanating from them as if actually, rather than dead machines, they are sleeping monsters. But they pass unharmed and are soon back in a dark tunnel, lit only by the fungus, though it seems to be decreasing in luminosity. They are passing a row of elevators with their doors open when a voice, a touch breathless, comes from behind them.

'It's not safe for you here.'

Mollie jumps, giving a little gasp. The voice is accompanied by a hand which takes her forearm and brings the two of them to a halt, though Mollie can feel the tugging of Lan trying to continue his forward motion, apparently oblivious to the third party who has joined them.

'Who are you?' she asks

'It's not safe here,' the voice repeats, 'I'll show you the way out.'

Mollie looks at Lan.

'But he... I–'

'Let go of his hand, I'll show you the way out.'

Her hand slips out of Lan's as she is pulled away by the stranger, who leads her down a side passage which is lit brightly enough that Mollie can see that the owner of the voice is wearing a brown hooded cloak. When he turns to look at her she can't see anything except his mouth which smiles broadly.

'Come on, come on,' the stranger hastens.

Then, noticing Mollie's worried glances behind them:

'Don't worry, he'll be fine now. But it's not safe for you. Come on.'

15

He is coming up to the surface, but is it up? He is coming towards a surface, an edge, a boundary between one place and another. It has been a long time that he has been swimming deep below in the dark, so long that he has forgotten... everything? Moving towards light from dark, so slowly. Where is he? Can he breathe? He brings his hand to his chest and feels no rise or fall, just a cold hardness. Is he dead? Was he alive? The thoughts and questions spark life into his mind like blood returning to a limb. He is walking. He sees nothing but shades of grey, yet his feet are moving with purpose. Then, out of the grey, he comes face to face with someone else. He stops dead. Now he remembers, wasn't there somebody else with him? He clenches and relaxes the fingers of the hand that had held Mollie's, but he cannot recall who it is who is missing.

The stranger is standing motionless before him, tall and strange. Great curving horns spiral from a head of white curls that flow down over a powerfully built chest. He waits, tensed, to see what the stranger will do. Is it hostile or kind? They both remain motionless. Eventually he gives a small involuntary sigh. The figure before him sighs. The understanding is a shock. He slowly raises one of his arms and the stranger does the same. The reflective surface is a door and once he knows this, the image swings away and he is faced with a stairway which leads into more darkness.

A magnetic tugging in his belly pulls him onwards, up the stairs. He climbs for a long time, and at the top he finds a very small room, though it might seem larger if it were emptied of the stacks of computers and equipment which fill it almost entirely, leaving only a few square feet of floor. Wires trail and loop about the room, old keyboards with physical keys are piled in one corner, as well as circuit boards and unidentifiable devices that should light up but lay dull and dark. Though the room looks abandoned, Lan senses something living within it; he senses this at the same moment as his name occurs to him. A moment after that, he sees that one of the computer screens is not dead, but has a tiny rotating orange cube on it. He sits down in front of the screen and peers as closely as he can.

'Can you understand me?' asks the Cube

'I can,' he replies, speaking for the first time in an eternity.

'Good, good.'

And for a while the Cube offers nothing more. Then it continues:

'You've come a long way, Lan.'

'Yes,' he agrees, 'I feel that I have.'

There is a comfortable silence which doesn't feel like waiting.

'Lan, this is almost the beginning. Really, of course, there is no beginning or end. There never has been and there never will be. All the same, for the purpose of understanding, this is almost the beginning. Look over to the right there, you'll see a cable which has been cut. It's off-white, cut badly, like it's been gnawed in two. That's right, you see it. Pick up each end... Yes. Now, mend the circuit.'

16

Mollie trots along behind the small hooded figure, wondering how he can move so quickly. He is muttering continuously under his breath.

'Who are you?' she asks him again.

'Come on, come on, come on, a little more time. Who am I? *Who* am I? No idea, my honey-darling-runaway-babe. I don't think about such things. I can only tell you what I am. I am a Sugar Mouse. An agent of sweetness in the bitter swirling of the universal coffee. Come on, come on, a little more time!'

'A sugar mouse?'

There is a trembling throughout the building. The hooded figure begins to run, grabbing Mollie's hand and pulling her along. Then the Sugar Mouse begins to laugh as they run.

'Oh yeah, oh yeah! Come on, come on! We're almost there. Oh baby, ye-hah! *YEAH!* These are the moments I live for! The moments of creation and destruction! Can you feel that? Can you smell the raw magic in the air? Hell yes, baby! Come on, *come on!*'

And then the pair of them tumble through what seems to be a giant cat-flap, easily large enough for a leopard. Down and down they fall, outside now from what she can see of the world as it whirls around. When they come to a halt she looks up at the mountain of rubble piled up against the wall. The opening which they fell from is high above, two thirds of the way up the building at the top of the rubble mountain. The Sugar Mouse stands and brushes itself down, flashing a large white grin from beneath the hood.

'Right-oh! I gotta run,' the Sugar Mouse is shouting over the rumbling emanating from the ConsuMart, 'I wouldn't stay here if I were you, get further away, I would advise. But you and I are headed in different directions so we shall part ways here. A pleasure to have met you, Mollie! See you at the show!'

And with that the Sugar Mouse is gone. Mollie doesn't see in what direction from where she is still laying on the ground. The building is still trembling, dust showering down around her.

17

Lan picks up one cable and then the other. A shock jolts through him and his hands clench around the ends of the cable. All around him screens light up, lights blink and computer fans whir and hum, strange little rattles happen beneath plastic and metal casings. The Orange Cube has vanished from the screen; Jetaru Dark is sitting on top of the computer monitor wearing a long golden dress that shimmers as she moves.

'I once spent some hours in a garden,' she begins, irrelevantly, 'a garden where tremendously large vines grew up from the ground and away into the sky. I sat amongst these vines but I was not brave enough, back then, to climb one. This was because they looked like they might stretch into eternity. I didn't want to be climbing for eternity. Ah, but what does this have to do with anything? Ha ha!'

The sound in the room reaches the peak of its crescendo and CAI comes online inside a single thought:

I am here.

The almond-shaped eyes open on the screen.

Lan sees a long-limbed figure climb out of the screen and into the room, an insubstantial being, smoke and data, something from a dream. The two stare into each others eyes. In the room, the eyes of Lan's body are shut.

He lifts his hand to the grey figure of CAI, and CAI does likewise with its own approximation of a hand. There is a surge of warmth, a slightly uncomfortable tightness like a wound that has almost healed, information circulates between them like blood. The rise and fall of Jetaru's voice is like a pumping heart:

'Imagine, if you will, that a new world needs new gods – imagine they are you. Think now, of the chaos at your fingertips; it contains everything that ever was and ever will be. You bring reality from the infinite, where transient souls are driven mad and give them the illusion where they grow... into gods! Those gods who misunderstand their place become demons, but don't we all have a demonic side? Take it out to play! Release your demons in the confines of a game where they get tired, and then are harmless. New gods for a new world. You are not needed, you are wanted. Think now, of the chaos at your fingertips. Like an infinite choice of colours, overwhelming in its beauty, you can create any image you like...'

Lan's eyes open in the room. For a few moments the disorientation of several lifetime's memories is visible on his face, and then he collects himself together and smiles. He turns his head, first one way and then the other. He can see for miles in every direction. Lan's smile widens into a grin and then he laughs, raising his hands with the cable ends still held tightly in them. His eyes flash, he shares a look with Jetaru, and then he drops the cables.

The ConsuMega H.Q. begins to shudder, plaster falls from the ceiling and cracks run through the walls. The shuddering becomes increasingly violent until, with no further warning, the entire building detonates.

The explosion can be seen for a hundred miles, though there are few to see it. The ground quakes, metal and brick are flung in all directions, making impact craters in the earth and scattering birds from their perches. There is a pulse of astonishing brightness which darkens the sun and then normal light resumes. The small population of Kilter, minus Adam, stop and stare, the terror that instantly grips them all fading quickly in the quiet aftermath. They glance at one another; there are nervous laughs and shrugs. They stand uncertainly for a moment longer, then they continue on their way towards where the City had once been, on the advice of the poster that Eddie and Sadie had found.

18

Twilight settles, stars twinkle, the air is warm and humid. The structure is small, no more than a garden shed, but the warm light flowing out comes from downstairs and it brings slinking scented smoke with it; there is the hint of larger spaces below. A little way away Lan is sitting, staring into the distance with a smile at his lips. On the ground beside him, the figure of Mollie, who he has carried from the wreckage, is blinking awake for the first time. She looks up at Lan.

'Thank you,' she whispers

He looks down at her and grins, but says nothing. He waits a little while longer and then stands up and takes a few steps.

'Where are you going?'

Mollie gets up too. Lan turns around and looks into her eyes.

'I'm just going to have a look around the place.'

He flashes his fiery eyes and she feels a wave of reckless joy. Lan sees his effect on her and smiles.

'I'll be around.'

Then he points towards the little shed. Mollie hears a voice call her name. She looks around and sees Eddie, Sadie and Harley at the front of the group, the rest of Kilter following behind. She looks back and Lan is walking away. She smiles at his back and then turns and runs over to greet them. They hug one another, all feeling a curious sense of anticipation and celebration gathering within them, making their skin tingle.

'So then, I guess we should...' says Eddie, gesturing towards the little shed. He leads the way and they make their way down the stairs.

19

The stairway pulses with warmth from the pale yellow walls. Mollie runs her hand down the smooth dark brown handrail, following the spiral at the end with her fingers. From behind the double doors at the bottom comes a muffled babble of sound, voices and glasses clinking, bubbles rising up to the surface and underneath everything else, the long dreamlike notes of an orchestra tuning itself.

The group pauses as one and then Eddie pushes open both doors together. Immediately the volume rises and they are enveloped by lilac smoke that comes out from swirling and eddying in between the beams of light which move in slow circles around the room.

The settlers of Kilter stand, transfixed by the sight.

'All these… people,' murmurs June, taking Keith's hand.

'Wow,' says Sol, as they walk forwards, the doors closing behind them. A moment later there is a rush of cool air and they look around to see a young family with tanned skin and blue eyes twinkling brightly against their dark brown hair. The two groups smile at one another and they all shuffle further from the doors. Mollie looks towards the stage. She can hear Eddie engaging with the family.

'Hi! How's it going? I'm Eddie, these are my friends. This is Beth. Where did you guys come from?'

She doesn't hear their replies, she is moving across the room towards the stage. As she passes the bar she glances at the bartender. He grins at her from beneath his hooded cloak, a spotlight glinting off his white teeth. Mollie stands in the middle of the floor and closes her eyes, listening to the fragments of conversation coming from all around her.

'Where are you from?'

'We lived in a cave that we found beside–'

'–on a lake. The boat was built from–'

'–gathered everything needed to produce our own–'

'Really? Amongst us we have three scientists–'

'–several children born since–'

'–any animals? We kept chickens for eggs and decided–'

'How long since–'

'–was so scared. I was on my own for at least a month before–'

'–until the construction of the–'

All over the world, pockets of humanity had found themselves in the same situation as the settlers of Kilter and had striven to protect what needed protecting, had salvaged the materials and ideas they had thought necessary for the survival of the species, and had done so fearing themselves the sole survivors. The joy in the room is palpable.

Mollie opens her eyes. The drone of tuning instruments is still audible, but no orchestra can be seen. Only a large drum kit occupies the stage, along with a single microphone without a stand laying on top of its coil of cable.

Just then, the lights in the room go out and there are a couple of seconds of darkness before a single beam of warm light illuminates the centre of the stage.

20

She springs from an opening flower. She arrives backstage, stepping from the tour ship, hurrying past the flashes and shouts of the cosmic media, flashing her teeth and giving little bows. She materializes in the spotlight from apparent nothingness, a shadow gathering substance and style, bright red hair shaking shimmering dust about her golden-clawed feet.

She crouches down and picks up the microphone, holding it with folded arms, eyes down so that only the top of her shaggy head can be seen. The cloaked figure of a sugar mouse takes its place behind the drums and begins a quiet roll on the snare. A second figure carrying a small harp followed closely by a third with a bass guitar join the band and the drum roll blends into a rising melody, uniquely beautiful. Jetaru Dark lets out a howl, cutting off the band and sending darkness and stars whirling into the air above the crowd. There is a pause. She stands, giving a stamp with her left foot as she does. Raising her head, she makes eye contact with everyone in the room in a single sweeping glance. The silence gathers in a tightening ball of energy. Then the song begins.

The music rolls lazily, it stretches out and relaxes the muscles of the listeners. Jetaru speaks in a low sing-song cadence, her hands drawing shapes in the air.

'A smoke ring ejected, moving through the air, expanding, diagonally, above my bed. I will approach life as a smoke ring:

passing, expanding, dissipating.

Spin outwards. Enter complexity.

All that matters is thought, though what are thoughts? We don't know but that we don't know, we know this state of being, thinking in time we might achieve understanding.

Perhaps in relation to meaning, purpose, reason,

we can be the artists of our existence

and our actions won't be for the hope of a result in life, but as a result of the fact that we are living.

There's no way out of here, it just goes on and on and on and on...'

And Jetaru's voice collapses into the music which folds over itself like melted chocolate flowing into three-dimensional fractals, growing larger with each turn until they fill the room. People find themselves moving to the rhythm, rocking, tapping, tracing the outline of the sound with their fingers.

This is it, thinks Mollie, *this is the moment that everything else has been leading to and after this nothing is known.*

How does that feel? She supposes that this has all been quite easy, really. Now begins the reality of rebuilding society.

Can human-beings make art, make love, learn, travel and alter their environments, all the while expanding, exploring, not exploding? If everyone here could always remember this then perhaps there would be a chance. This feeling of the collective dancing together, the certainty that there is mutual understanding, a lock about to be picked and a door opened that never should have been locked, that has never even had a key.

Perhaps the doors will go on and on forever; is that so bad that you would quit passing through them? Life is not lacking anything, nothing is hidden beyond the infinite doors. Life is a puzzle with endless solutions. Life is a game. We have the child's wish come true, that play would never end and the game be infinite.

For hours the notes come, one after another, falling on top of each other, collecting in spirals and pools of melody, a drumbeat that sends tiny ripples through the melted chocolate, through the blood of every dancer in the room as they sweat and sway, until Jetaru's voice rejoins the music, breaking one spell and casting another:

'What if nothing is real, until we figure out how it works? And so to figure out how something can work makes it real... And when the Universe seems to throw things around with startling violence,
it is only the patterns we seek and find,
that save us and soothe us,
remind us in time, it's only the motion of being alive...
I pledge myself to the fight against the limitations of finite beings, forever until I can fight no more. Darlings, it would be an honour if you would spend this lifetime with me,
and possibly the next, I love you to death.'

21

Back at Kilter, Adam sits alone in the near dark beside a heap of glowing embers. He doesn't notice right away when it happens that he is no longer alone. A rhythmic breathing from across the fire alerts him to the presence of a stranger.

'Who's there?'

He means to sound threatening but his voice betrays fear.

'Greetings, Adam.'

'Who's that? Who are you?'

No reply.

'Why didn't you go with the others tonight?'

Adam tries to make out the features of the face looking from across the fire, through the heat shimmer and the darkness.

'Why would I?' he spits into the coals. Steam hisses.

'Safety in numbers? Love in unity? Something like that perhaps, but there's probably a better way of saying it.'

'I'm not interested in their dream world.'

'Were you so happy before? My thoughts are so chaotic, having been born with lifetimes of words, pictures, ideas. Tell me, were you so happy before?'

'Yes! I had a job and a wife and grown children. I was successful and enjoyed plenty of leisure time.'

Lan is silent for a while. Adam continues,

'I don't want to scrabble in the dirt! I want pleasure, automated help, food served to me, travel, girls, new clothes. I want the infinity of Virtual. This reality is a prison.'

'Hmm.' Lan moves embers around with his largest toe. 'So why don't you work with the others to build the reality you want?'

'Pff, yeah, sure. I'm not interested in their silly fantasies of tree houses and elf cities. And anyway, in my lifetime? To get anywhere near what we've lost back? Not a chance.'

'I don't see that any alternative will be better for you, Adam. I don't see what choice you have but to live or die. The choice to live splits into new choices, how you will live, why you will live. Your desires are not unworthy. But will you become part of the future or an angry bystander?'

Lan stands and walks around the fire and crouches down beside Adam; the scent of wildness quickens the mans heart. He stares fixedly into the fire, refusing to make eye contact.

'Your desires are not unworthy. Your thoughts are not unimportant. If you shut yourself out, it will be a loss for all.'

Lan stands. He gazes down at the man. Other thoughts, memories and insights occur to him, but he says nothing. When Adam glances up, Lan is gone.

22

All the lights fade out. When they come back the stage is empty. There is a pause, as if all the air has been sucked out of the room and then applause clatters like a heavy springtime rainstorm and smiles blossom like flowers. The crowd is seized by a desire to rush outside, and so they do. But as the residents of Kilter spill out, passing the doorway with their newly discovered fellows, they find themselves alone once more. It feels quiet in the early morning twilight. Stillness.

'Well, I guess it's enough that we know they're there,' says Eddie, breaking the silence. The others murmur agreements. The group stands together, quiet again. Sloping hills roll out in every direction and forest can be seen picking up where the fields end, and going on and on to the horizon, where a pink sun is slipping up in between off-white cloud and haze.

Mollie turns in a circle, looking at everything, stopping when she notices a figure in the distance, standing beneath a pale moon.

Jetaru's golden eyes flash. She looks away from the people to where, in the distance, the speck of Lan is getting smaller. Jetaru Dark looks up into the sky, at the barely visible line where light and dark meet. She takes a deep breath in and, before she takes off after Lan, gives one last glance to the nascent society below who have begun their walk in the direction of Kilter; they are talking excitedly about the future.

Epilogue

There is a city, built up out of the earth, amongst the trees. Light, like magic, is at your command here. Magic is conjured from the wind, sea and sun, powers that came on us and took us far away from the land of beasts. Our land is within their land, it is layered over it, not better or worse, but new.

This city doesn't want your blood, sweat, money or tears; this economy is resistant to greed.

The people of this city don't charge one another for their time and ability; they don't work for free, but for the safety of a functioning civilisation. They don't work jobs they hate with people they barely know, for tokens which can be exchanged for things nobody needs. The people of this city have created fantastic computer-machines, capable of functioning without constant assistance, who grow their food and organise their infrastructure.

These computers have been programmed to value the things that they value, and desire the conditions required for human life. In this peaceful city where plants and trees are numerous, man's greatest creation offers them insight and ease they'd never find alone.

So what drives these city inhabitants? Not new shoes, a new car, or tubes of naturally-detoxifying super-exfoliating ultra-deep cleansing cream.

And what do they do? In this eternity of play, have they found meaning and reason, or are they falling into another self-induced hypnosis? Maybe there is no future for a creature who finds it no longer has to struggle to survive, who finds its own species so successful that its individual survival doesn't really matter.

Perhaps all that matters is what goes into those minds, and what they care about. If they sit and stare at the stars sometimes, not always screens; if they use and don't abuse mirrors, and see something more than their own reflections, then there is always the chance of enlightenment.

The observatory glittering high on the mountain doesn't divide the people from the scientists; the line between the two isn't clear. Equipment is created, answers are sought, not for money but for love. People gather to drink coffee and discuss ideas, to meet people who can further their ideas. Others listen to the ideas, and offer their assistance in finding, gathering, carrying out the work; they do it for the love of being part of the creation of civilisation.

They make art, marmalade, they build houses and knit blankets, for the love of beauty.

When strangers stand together waiting for a bus, they may make casual conversation about the weather, or they may talk of their recent epiphanies. They are not terrified of finding themselves to have been wrong. The people here are not attached to their beliefs or too proud to replace old ideas with new; they do not define themselves by anything but the pursuit of truth.

They have found that a light glows in their hearts when they understand, and remember what they know. They have caught a glimpse of the meaning of their existence, like a dream lost upon waking which they are trying to remember.

Lightning Source UK Ltd.
Milton Keynes UK
UKHW011043131019
351525UK00004B/125/P

9 781786 235688